Doubting Thomas

ATLE NÆSS

Doubting Thomas
A Novel about Caravaggio

Translated from the Norwegian by Anne Born

PETER OWEN
London

Translated by Anne Born from the Norwegian *Den Tvilende Thomas*

PETER OWEN PUBLISHERS
73 Kenway Road, London SW5 0RE

Peter Owen books are distributed in the USA by Dufour Editions Inc.,
Chester Springs, PA 19425-0007

First published in Great Britain 2000
This paperback edition 2002

Translation © Anne Born 2000
© Atle Næss 1997

ISBN 0 7206 1151 2

A catalogue record for this book is available from the British Library.

Printed and bound in Great Britain by Bookmarque Ltd, Croydon, Surrey

Contents

Editor's Preface

ON 26 MAY 1606, on the Campo Marzio (the Field of Mars) in Rome, the painter Michel Angelo Merisi da Caravaggio killed a man by the name of Ranuccio Tomassoni. Caravaggio had already been arrested on a number of occasions for various reasons before: violence, assault, illegally bearing arms, general trouble-making, defamation. At the same time he was, without question, regarded as the leading painter of his time in Rome, probably in Italy and possibly in the whole of Europe. He specialized in ecclesiastical art, particularly altar-pieces with biblical themes.

After the murder he fled from the Vatican City and was condemned to death *in absentia*. Several of his powerful patrons sought to have him acquitted, however, and their efforts succeeded in the summer of 1610. But, by the time Pope Paul V Borghese signed the reprieve, Caravaggio had already died, in mysterious circumstances.

In 1996 the records presented here were found in the *Archivio Segreto Vaticano,* more specifically in the *Archivio Borghese* [MS reg. no. 1276]. They are reproduced here *in extenso* in the editor's own translation; obvious spelling mistakes have been corrected, as have inconsistencies in the Latin phrases appearing here and there in the text. For stylistic reasons quotations from the Vulgate have been rendered with corresponding passages from the Authorized Version of the Bible of 1890.

It appears both directly and indirectly from these accounts that they were gathered for evidence in the Holy See's hearing of the case for a reprieve. They have the character of witnesses' statements, ordered by the office of the Curia. One of the narrators, one Innocenzo Promontorio, writes a longer and more detailed account than the others, and it could be tempting to assume that he had something to do with the collection of evidence. However, this theory runs into difficulty, something which will be commented on in the postscript where the authenticity and historical reliability of the records is assessed.

Rome

The Account of
Innocenzo Promontorio

I

IT IS THE route I always take. I follow St Peter's road to martyrdom, up the steep southern slope of the Gianicolo Hill where he
had to carry his cross. The little church lies there for that very
reason, built on the actual place where the Master's disciple was
nailed to the cross, which was then raised with his head down, in
accordance with his last request.

S. Pietro in Montorio. The whole city lies beneath me. The
lovely warm evening light brings grace to all the seediness; it illu-
minates all the hideous heathen ruins out in the Campagna and
brings out hundreds of shades of yellow and red in the densely
massed houses on both sides of the Tiber. But the churches and
palaces rear up like rocks, seamarks among the waves of roofs.

The Franciscans in the church here know me and they leave
me in peace. The little brothers walk around quietly, watch me
light a candle before the fresco of the flagellated Christ in the
side chapel just to the right of the door. They are well aware that
I do not come here to meditate on Peter's martyrdom, to follow
his road of suffering up the hill from Sta Maria della Scala on the

outskirts of the Trastevere and on here to the place where Peter fulfilled his calling and, in truth, became a rock.

It is quiet up here. The average Roman is not so strikingly pious that he takes the long – and hard – road hither. I can sit on the steps outside the church for as long as I like. The monks know I am here to pay homage to another martyrdom than that of Peter: that of ordinary sinful people, banal, humdrum. I recall sudden death and incomprehensible suffering, with none of the sublime significance that makes Peter's end convey both light and darkness, joy and pain.

The Franciscans say nothing. But they were the ones who took in the body of Beatrice Cenci and gave it a grave.

Our time is not a happy time.

The signs are clear enough. They can be seen even in the heavens. New stars appear, independent bodies strayed from the great Order; they portend unmistakeable chaos, war and earthquake. There are tales of blood-red crosses that suddenly become visible on people's feet, halfway up their ankles; in precisely the place where the nail was hammered into Christ's foot. The colour of the crosses changes into yellow before they disappear, without doubt a sign of coming plague and epidemic.

But we have no need of these signs. We do not even need the tales of patricide and *crimen bestialitatis*.* It is enough to go out on the streets and surreptitiously study the violent, immoral and dissolute life being played out there. Law-abiding citizens are

---

* Sexual intercourse with animals. (Editor's note)

defamed or even attacked and robbed. Virtuous women are assaulted while those who are fallen shamelessly offer themselves. Many will say that the six thousand years which Our Lord God in his divine mercy has been pleased to set as the limit for the age of the World is running out. The final result approaches; the last day, when a greater Judge shall put us in his scales and find us wanting.

I wish to state this firmly at the commencement of my account, since I am aware that my own share in it is not merely that of reporter. I myself have taken part in actions that unfortunately have added to the sum of vices, as has also my friend, he who is the subject of my writing. But if my account is to help anyone, it must hold to the truth. This is the story of a painter and a murder, but also of a man who lost his faith and found it again.

Consequently this account will not be concerned in the least with Beatrice Cenci. All the same it is for her that I write it. So let me begin by describing what happened on 12 February, AD 1599, all the more because my proper story in some respects begins on that date.

The grotesque ruins that still encircle our city are, according to what is thought, the remains of enormous structures built by the heathen emperors. Of all the misdeeds of these fearsome potentates the worst were undoubtedly those where they maltreated and killed good Christians, in vast spectacles with wild animals and professional fighters.

The princes of our day do nothing like this. Yet, all the same, the exercise of justice has become a kind of public performance. I know very well that this custom has a moral purpose. It sets out to show the populace the terrible consequences brought upon us by sin, not only in eternity but now in our imperfect earthly existence. The people must *see* the consequences of evil passions and actions, *hear* the shrieks of the sinners when justice strikes.

I shall say nothing here of Beatrice's guilt, particularly as all discussion of the reasonableness of the sentence was expressly forbidden, a ban which is still in force. Moreover, at the time I was perhaps completely unable to see any blame in her. She herself admitted under torture that she took part in planning the murder of her father, but maintained it was because he wished to commit unmentionable acts of violence against her, acts so totally *contra naturam* between father and daughter that they excused every imaginable defensive action. Perhaps things would have taken a different course if she had pleaded this at once. But she had denied all guilt and did not produce this explanation until the chief examiner slowly crushed her knuckles in the thumbscrew. Let me merely mention that no one had any doubt that Francesco Cenci was one of the worst scoundrels who ever took his unworthy steps on our fruitful Earth. If his family – and Beatrice among them – really planned his demise, they certainly committed a great crime, but it was not without reason.

I can feel my pen slip from my grasp. How I flinch from writing the few sentences to describe what happened on the Ponte Sant'Angelo that day in February. But first I must admit that I was not myself present. It was the painter, my former friend, who is to be the leading character in my account, who recounted it to me.

Even though all four of them – Signora Cenci and the three children – were condemned to death, it pleased His Holiness to pardon the youngest son, Bernardo, who was fifteen. But he was ordered to remain beside the scaffold and watch all the executions. It was intended that he should assist the executioner by handing him the axe, but he fainted so often that he was more dead than alive while it was all going on. Afterwards he was sent immediately to the galleys.

Never in our days has Rome seen so great a crowd. From the Palazzo Orsini to the Tor di Nona, indeed, right down to S. Giovanni de'Fiorentini, horses and carriages were packed close. At least four people were killed in the crush, some fell under the horses' hoofs and some were, quite simply, squashed to death. The crowd uttered threats when Beatrice, her mother Lucrezia and brother Giacomo were led out of the castle and on to the scaffold erected in the centre of the bridge. Some screamed 'Death to the patricide!' but most called out that she was innocent. It pains me deeply to say it, but taunts were even directed at His Holiness himself.

But Clemens VIII – blessed be his memory in eternity – was not present in person. He was celebrating a mass in S. Giovanni in Laterano for the souls of the condemned.

Well, to the point: Mother Lucrezia swooned. Some say she had already died of fright, and her head was parted from her body without further ado.

But Beatrice was alive, and all agree that in her pallor she was more beautiful than ever. She cried out that God must never forgive those who allowed this injustice, and the crowd responded to her in such an enraged manner that the soldiers on guard began to drive people back with force, causing even more to be hurt. Among these was my friend the painter, who received a blow on his shoulder from a club. The revolt was so violent that the executioner did not dare to delay further but forced the girl, who was still crying out, to her knees, with her hands bound behind her back.

Then he struck. My friend was so close he could see the blood gush out; and more, he swears that he could see Beatrice's expression *after* the beheading, how spasms of hate and contempt passed over her beautiful face as the head rolled down from the scaffold and over the bridge. The executioner left it there. He did not lift it up by the hair and hold it out to the crowd as is customary. It was as if he was afraid that the bloody head would go on calling out curses and excite the crowd still further.

But the sight had had its effect. The waves of the human sea no longer thundered. There were only a few faint cries when Giacomo was taken up, held firmly by four stout men and pinched with iron tongs made red hot on a small forge, so the smell of burned flesh merged with his cries of agony. Then he was dragged to the scaffold and thrown down. The executioner struck him several times on the head with a big wooden club. He might have died of that before his throat was cut, like the carcass of a beast. Then the body was divided into four and flung aside like bloody slaughterhouse refuse.

But shortly afterwards, when passage through the streets was clear again, Beatrice's body was fetched and brought here to the Franciscans of S. Pietro in Montorio, from where in the fullness of time her maltreated body will rise again. So she rests in consecrated earth. How this was possible I do not wish to enlarge upon.

II

Well, then. I heard all these monstrous details of the execution over countless glasses of grappa that same evening. Afterwards I vomited miserably in the gutter outside the inn and had to put up with not a little scornful jeering.

But when I woke up next morning I had not only landed in prison and was feeling a cohort of small devils playing havoc inside me, I had lost my faith in there being one indivisible truth.

From that night on, Ambiguity became my new God. And I did not have to search far before I found the symbols of my new divinity.

It is the popes themselves who have had the obelisks erected, and of course I do not worry about their decisions. But for impressionable souls, like myself at this time . . . Are they not extremely ambiguous signs, stretching a finger towards heaven in so many places here in the city? Ha, who says it is a *finger*? Learned folk maintain that the great stone phallus on the Piazza del Popolo was once raised in honour of the Sun God. Anyway it is a fact that Blessed Sixtus V, who instituted so many splendid initiatives for the renewal of the city, also had this colossus moved from what was the Circus Maximus of the heathens to the dominant position it now occupies, just outside the church where the revered and beautiful Madonna di Popolo is venerated by so many pious souls, a church which also has a part to play in the story of my friend the painter.

Ambiguity? It is true that His Holiness had this and the other obelisks sprinkled with holy water and adorned with a cross on the top. It is true that it must be a pleasing act, a triumph for the Church to convert the heathen monument; to force this index finger of the devil – or his sexual member – to draw attention to the Lord in his heaven.

But the signs on the sides of the colossus are still there, ominous images. They are not ordinary pictures; they hold a sombre meaning even though we cannot read them. How can we know that these signs, birds' heads, lions' bodies, do not hold some or other curse strong enough to be unaffected by any holy water and every prayer? How can we *know* it really is the Church that triumphs when these slender dark stones are erected in the most prominent squares in our Eternal City?

On the very square outside that St Peter's Church which now towers above the old Vatican meadows where the apostle finally found his grave – even *there* the good Sixtus placed one of these stone monsters. To be sure, this obelisk has no inscriptions, but is it not therefore equally ominous in its dark silence? As if that were not enough, His Holiness had to call out 900 workmen,

150 horses and forty-seven cranes to get the monster moved and erected. Even so, there was nearly a disaster; for it is told how Sixtus ordered the crowd of onlookers to keep absolute silence as it was raised under threat of sentence of death and how a sailor in the crowd saved the day by breaking the ban and calling out that they must dampen the ropes before they snapped.*

I ask myself whether this titanic effort might not have been better expended on something else – not because I doubt the Holy Father's judgement but because all human activity is a choice. Our actions are not presented to us by nature; when we execute *one,* we exclude another.

No, no. Now I am jumping around far too wildly in my account. I who used to praise myself for my clear brain, which comprehended things swiftly and put them in their correct context! I must go back to the *Osteria della Torretta* near the Via della Scrofa where I heard the description of the executions and then drank myself senseless.

It was my friend the painter Michel Angelo da Merisi who depicted the horrific scenes on the Ponte Sant'Angelo, who now intrudes into my account in earnest.

Merisi is the family name. He was probably given the name of the angel from someone who knew the excitable tendencies of the Merisis in the hope that it might give the bearer a calmer cast

---

* It is said that the sailor and his family were rewarded by being given the sole right to supply St Peter's with palm branches every Palm Sunday, and thus laid the foundations for the palm production industry of Bordighera, but modern research rejects this story. (Editor's note)

of mind. In which case it was hardly the name of the warlike leader of the hosts of heaven he should have been dubbed with.

For that matter, most people now just call him Caravaggio after the small town near Bergamo from where the family hail.

The painter is not a big man. At the time of the execution of Beatrice Cenci he was not yet thirty years old. His slim, lithe figure is in constant movement, so full of restlessness that he cannot sit quietly at a table – indeed, even when he paints, his movements are singularly impetuous. His face is not remarkable – presumably women like him because of his *gaze*, from the dark brown eyes in the restless features that come to rest and *look*. It is the gaze of a painter, which makes things he sees remain visible for ever. Women see themselves in that gaze, I think, or the dream of themselves. And his eyes are all the more compelling because he has big, beautifully arched eyebrows, which almost form a semicircle. His hair – when I last saw him – was quite long, thick and slightly curly, although seldom well-combed; and at that time he had just a moustache and a rather well-groomed goatee, which could not hide the sensual mouth.

Anna Bianchini was with us that evening. She did not like me but tolerated my company for the sake of sitting at the same table as Michel. I knew quite well why she did not care for me; it was because of a foolish business a year or two earlier when Michel, the painter Prospero Orsi and I were sitting in an inn together. Anna came in with two women friends. Michel glanced at them with that gaze of his and remarked *sotto voce*: 'Look at Anna. What a lovely arse she has!'

But Anna heard what he said, perhaps that was intentional. However it was, she turned towards us and said aloud: 'Maybe, painter, you *too* have a lovely arse, that *I* am not allowed to get my hands on . . .'

Michel took it quietly, but I stood up, went over and gave Anna a box on the ear. That is not the sort of thing a man can allow himself in a public place. Anna looked as if she was about to fly at me, but instead mine host appeared – in fact, he was her pimp at the time – and said we had all better simmer down or we would be asked to leave.

But after that Michel and the red-haired Anna established a kind of friendship. He used her as his model several times. It was not hard to see that she loved the painter, although perhaps not in the down-to-earth way in which she practised her trade – I don't know much about that. On that evening when we sat drinking grappa after the executions on the Ponte Sant'Angelo, I couldn't help thinking of the *The Penitent Magdalen*.

That is certainly a painting with a double meaning: Anna as Magdalene, the model as reality, the whore disguised as a whore – or maybe we were the only ones who saw the picture like this, we who knew the artist and his model. It is a serene picture, rather different from later paintings by Michel, with no trace of that wild, slashing light of his. The skin colour of Anna's neck and face is in subdued, golden tones. Her beautiful red hair is in shadow, her silk blouse falls lightly and tenderly around her, her damask dress is in shades of brown and gold. Only the scarlet cloak she wears, half enveloped in it for protection, is really dramatic, almost tangibly bringing guilt and sin into the picture. And then the expression on her face, the lowered gaze, so gentle but moved by a great sorrow.

That was the picture. But Anna Bianchini, the little whore, she was no repentant Magdalene as she sat at our table the day Beatrice Cenci's head rolled across the Ponte Sant'Angelo. Even after many years in Rome her Sienese accent could still be discerned in her speech. *She* had not been on the bridge watching the executions. She had been about her work. After a show like that the customers went wild, she told us. They stood in queues outside the brothels. And the violence continued inside: frantic men threw themselves over the women as if the sight of rolling heads, blood and fresh entrails had sent them into a fleshly intoxication, whipped up their passions to ecstasy. Several of the whores had had to call for their pimps because they feared for their lives.

Ah, yes, Anna Bianchini, I remember you that way with such melancholy, you little whore, you, with a blue mark on your throat put there by a bloodlusting client who demanded to strangle you during the act, or at least pretend to. Moral conduct in our hallowed Rome, the capital of Christianity, leaves a lot to be desired. Evil tongues – and there are plenty of those – believe it is due to the great surplus of *men* in our town. Here are not only cardinals and prelates by the score, those who have dedicated their lives to the Virgin and no other woman, here also are all kinds of representatives, informants and messengers from all the Italian states and courts, as well as from the furthest countries.

But that was the stuff you lived on, poor little redhead!

Incidentally there are other reasons than the excessive intoxication to make me still remember that night even so long afterwards. For it was the night I met both Phyllida Melandroni and Ranuccio Tomassoni – and went to prison for the first time in my life.

III

As I said, I vomited miserably into the gutter after the grappa, after Michel's descriptions of the executions and Anna's stories of bloodthirsty customers who set upon her with their *gladii seminis*[*] as if they wanted to split her in two with actual newly honed swords.

But I was not allowed to go home afterwards. Anna and Michel, he still cursing over the pain in his shoulder from the blow he had received, dragged me along through the town to the Via Condotti. It was about two hours after Ave Maria, so we could have been stopped by the police at any moment. Michel carried a sword without permission and Anna was a prostitute and thus not allowed to show herself in the street at that time of day. But both of them were unruly and drunk, walking along arm in arm singing bawdy songs as if they just had to arouse attention.

Even from two blocks away we heard the din from Phyllida Melandroni's house. We knocked, but it took a long time before

---

[*] Swords of the seed, a metaphorical expression for the penis. (Editor's note)

anyone inside reacted. Meanwhile the two of them went on singing, Michel in a clear high tenor which carried well through the night.

At last Phyllida came out.

At that time Signorina Melandroni was a woman in her mid-twenties, I would guess, although I must admit that my ability to judge a woman's age is not great. It is especially hard in prostitutes, who make use of all kinds of rejuvenating tricks and devices because of the nature of their trade. She was of medium height and well-built; she had masses of brown hair which she set up but which left her ears free. She wore heavy ear rings, each with a cluster of small pearls, like a provocative protest against the *Law Regarding Extravagance and Luxury*. When Michel announced who we were and why we had come she did not lower her gaze, as one might expect, but looked me straight in the face with clear greenish-brown eyes, the left one with a slight squint.

For Michel said: 'See here, Phyllida, this wreck is my friend Innocenzo. I've brought him along to you so you can liberate him from his name!'

'No, tonight we're enjoying ourselves,' said Phyllida amiably. 'He'd better come back in working hours!'

There were three men in the house. I knew one of them, the architect Onorio Longhi, Michel's best friend. The other two were obviously brothers.

They were both above medium height and powerfully built, with long brown hair. The eldest had several scars on his beardless face, like those I had seen on war veterans. Both wore daggers in their belts.

Their names were Giovan Francesco and Ranuccio Tomassoni. Giovan was the eldest and most unassuming, Ranuccio behaved as if he was in his own home.

More drinks went round and they talked about war. Onorio Longhi had been a military architect in Flanders, Giovan Francesco a captain in the ill-fated campaign against the heathen Turks, from which only a couple of thousand souls returned out of an army of more than seven thousand. But the captain was not one of the garrulous kind. It was Longhi who talked; he went into details about soldiers with the top of their heads cut off, with crushed legs and their guts hanging out. He described how the enemy used linked cannon-balls: they whirled through the air like the sickle of Death incarnate, cutting down everything that came in their way.

Onorio was a good, if somewhat noisy and long-winded narrator. But Giovan Francesco grew even more silent, merely mumbled a few words about great desolate marshes, about trains that stuck fast so that provisions never arrived, about comrades drained by dysentery of strength and life in the most degrading manner.

Only when the silent soldier got up and left, while his brother stayed on, did I realize that Ranuccio was Phyllida's friend and protector. Then I also noticed how the prostitute's eyes clung to the face of my friend Michel the painter. At that point Longhi the architect was reciting poems he had written himself, Anna Bianchini was asleep in an adjoining room and Michel was attempting to sing to my somewhat wavering lute accompaniment.

Then the police arrived, and my friendship with the painter Michel Angelo Merisi da Caravaggio brought me into contact with the rats and cockroaches of the Tor di Nona's cellars for the first time. Sadly, it was not to be the last.

IV

The next day was Ash Wednesday. The carnival was well and truly over. Outside Sta Maria della Pace, where the statue of the Virgin had once started to bleed after having been struck by a stone thrown by a blasphemer, people were on their way to early Mass to have ash crosses drawn on their foreheads. I, too, felt rather penitent, but that was *inside* my forehead. I tried to get some meaning out of what the gaoler had said when he set us free. His Excellency Francesco Maria Bourbon del Monte, cardinal and representative at the Holy See for the Grand Duke Ferdinando de'Medici of Tuscany, was a keen art collector, and I knew he had bought several pictures from Michel. But why should he pay the fines for Michel's foolish actions?

And, above all, why should this great man pay *my* fines?

Trade was already under way at the Navona market. The fast had begun and the busy weeks had arrived for the fishmongers; there were pomfret and tench, eels, herring and cod, and a merchant with good connections in the south had conjured up both swordfish and goldmouth, which looked fresh and appetizing. I also noticed fine fat frogs and naturally the dried stockfish that we pay the earth to buy from Scandinavia to vary the diet during the weeks of fasting.

I was hungry. We elbowed our way through the crowded market and went down the little side street until we were outside the Palazzo Madama.

The proud building *stared* down on us with its severe rows of windows on four imposing storeys. But Michel did not even look up. He simply opened the door and nodded to the servant who came running up and showed us the way.

A new painting by Michel hung in the cardinal's study. *Love Victorious* was a handsome young boy. The lines of the picture ran together in his naked, emphasized but still childish, fleshly adornment, so that the god – or the boy – seemed naked to the point of being obtrusive. Apart from this, it was a superb painting. The boy's breast and stomach, not to mention his round, powerful thighs, were modelled as if by a sculptor. His face was vivid and lively, his half smile could be interpreted as both diffident and challenging. Around this Cupid lay, carelessly thrown, almost flung away, musical instruments, books and pieces of armour: thus love conquers all other earthly activities.

It was a disturbing picture to find in a room devoted to a cardinal's solemn profession. But it showed without doubt that del Monte was a connoisseur, one who valued pictures for how they were painted and not for the theme, as simple souls do.

'One of my men informed me last night about the commotion in the Via Condotti,' said the cardinal. 'Really, my friends – a drunken brawl in the house of a whore!'

'In a pseudo-smart quarter of limp pricks and torpid cunts,' replied Michel calmly. 'Someone must have tipped *gli sbirri** a wink. We weren't brawling more than usual. I didn't even start a fight with those whoresons from Terni.'

'I take it you mean the Tomassoni brothers, painter,' said del Monte, somewhat sharply but not disapprovingly.

'Just a couple of them. Incidentally, they're still sitting in the Tor di Nona as food for the cockroaches.'

'They are Farnese's men,' said the cardinal. 'The Devil can take care of his own. I have more than enough to do with my own villains.'

There I attempted to break in to thank del Monte for setting me free as well, but he interrupted me.

'I intend to carry out a Christian good deed,' he said. 'I shall rescue you two rascals from disgrace and ruin by taking you in here at the Palazzo Madama. You will get accommodation and food as trusted servants and, naturally, payment as usual for services – for you, Michel, that will be for your paintings. We cannot have you running around the streets in this manner any more. You will land in the galleys before we know it, and what will become of those soft painter's hands when your back is subjected to the whip to keep you in time with the huge oars, do you think?'

Michel raised his beautiful rounded eyebrows.

---

* Popular or vulgar: cops. (Editor's note)

'Is this an offer, cardinal? Do we have any choice?'

'Yes, the cellars beneath the Tor di Nona,' said del Monte. 'Or, since I do have some slight influence, I could try to get you transferred to Sant'Angelo. It may well be drier, but the screams of the tortured and those condemned to death can be somewhat trying, I have heard.'

'But what about me?' I managed to put in. 'Your Reverence, since I am not a painter or an artist, I don't know what service I can render instead . . .'

'To begin with, you shall journey to Padua, young man,' said the cardinal. 'Although I think a little food would be a good thing first. And a little wine. In truth, I believe the bodily humours are still seriously unbalanced, in both of you.'

V

From my habitual viewpoint by S. Pietro in Montorio I can see the wonderful dome of the ancient building of Sta Maria ad Martyres, which the old heathens, we are told, called the Pan Theon, the temple of all the gods. Taking a bearing from it, I can easily find the Palazzo Madama among all the roofs and can figure out the position of the Piazza Navona, down among the buildings just beyond it.

I did go to Padua, while the painter from Caravaggio moved into the cardinal's house. So for the following year I had to rely on reports and sporadic visits to the city to keep up with my friend's truly remarkable career.

But I had not even left when Michel was arrested early in

May. His offence was carrying a sword on the open street without the necessary permission and, in addition, he had another dangerous weapon that the policeman described as 'a very large pair of compasses'. In his defence Michel pleaded that he was 'one of del Monte's men' and therefore had a right to bear arms whenever he wished with the permission of his distinguished protector. This was enough to procure his liberty, except that the compasses were about to cause him greater difficulties than the sword.

It cannot be denied that Michel Angelo, despite his angelic name, was choleric and most often far too full of yellow bile. He had a particular aversion to the Academy of St Luke.

Here, unfortunately, I must insert a pair of blockheads into my account. The distinguished patron of the Academy was Cardinal Federico Borromeo. At this time the institution was run by the painter Federico Zuccari, an utter fool if ever one graced our city. Zuccari invoked not only the authority of the Church but also of the great Raphael's in support of his academy, and he painted an altar-piece for the academy church ready for the opening. The painting shows the patron saint of artists, the Blessed Luke, engaged in painting the Mother of God.

He might have got away with it if he had not had the incredible impudence to announce his facile smears as – a newly discovered Raphael!

And such trumpery was, unfortunately, supported by Cardinal Borromeo, who went to the Palazzo Madama a few days after Michel was arrested on the street and then released.

His mission was the large compasses, a weapon which had obviously both terrified and amazed the wretched *sbirro*. Michel had explained that they were purely and simply one of the tools of his trade. They were what was known as conversion compasses, which he used for transferring distances and measurements from his model directly on to the canvas.

Del Monte commanded me to be present, as this could be useful for me. But Michel himself was strictly ordered to make himself scarce.

The cardinal bade us consider the serious problems that could arise if one merely relied on scrutiny. In the most extreme and unpleasant cases this would lead to pure heresy, he pointed out, because man in his self-importance relies unconditionally on his lamentably imperfect senses, his so-called 'observations'. But in his arrogance the wretched human being could forget – or not wish – to compare these observations with those of the philosophers, the teaching of the Church and the lucid words of God. In passing he might mention the regrettable episode of a certain Giordano Bruno from Nola – undoubtedly an extremely gifted man but so unfortunately obstinate when it came to those very 'observations' – who at that moment found himself deep down in Castel Sant'Angelo awaiting a highly uncertain fate. In short – without going so far as to say that the same rules held good for the artist as for the natural scientist – he, the cardinal, would be so bold as to suggest to his honoured colleague, del Monte, the dangers of depending too slavishly on the earthly and imperfect in one's efforts to create beauty, as these conversion compasses could indicate that the painter Michel Merisi possibly did.

'Let us look at one of his pictures,' growled del Monte.

He led the cardinal and me into an adjoining room. There hung Michel's *St Catherine of Alexandria.*

The wise and pious woman was clad in a black velvet dress, and not even a Borromeo could fail to admire how Michel had caught the play of light and shadow in the folds of the dress. The blessed martyr knelt on a red silk cushion beside the spiked wheel, that frightful instrument with which the enemies of the Faith had tried to slay her and which she had so miraculously survived, if credence can be given to the reports. In her hand she held the sword that would finally implement her death, but in front of her lay a whip as a sign of the torture and pains she would have to undergo after she had converted, with the aid of her god-given wisdom, no less than fifty heathen philosophers.

Catherine herself was young and beautiful. Borromeo examined her face more closely. I hoped fervently it did not strike him that her gaze seemed to be directed straight at the viewer or that a somewhat more modest attitude would have suited better with Catherine's virginal mind.

But it was a brilliantly fine painting. Even though I felt I had been placed in an embarrassing situation, I saw how vitally alive this painted woman was. How can I explain it? She was not *painted* as a holy woman. She *was* a woman, but so convincingly there in her holy presence that she must draw every viewer to prayer and pious reflection.

Nevertheless, I thought of that cellar beneath Sant'Angelo and felt my hands tremble slightly.

'A good painting?' asked del Monte.

Borromeo crossed himself solemnly and bowed his head before Catherine's pure and beautiful face under the delicate halo.

'Painted to my commission,' said del Monte, pleased.

'Yes, yes, excellent,' responded the cardinal, clearing his throat. 'Think over what I have said, and remember I am not speaking in my own interest. Pass it on to Merisi the painter.'

'This young man will see to that,' del Monte nodded in my direction. 'He is himself a natural scientist and knows something about observations.'

'Hm, I see!' said Borromeo. 'I hope they also know something about God's clear word, both the painter and his young friend here.'

With that he left. I stayed on in front of the Blessed Catherine, who with her mild gaze promised me access to the wisdom of Heaven. I grew dizzy, as if the picture on the wall there had suddenly revealed a hidden danger, a deadly trap for the innocent viewer.

For Catherine's beautiful face did not belong to any blameless saint. It was the face of Phyllida Melandroni.

VI

At this point in my account I must insert a brief statement of a personal nature, for which I crave pardon.

I was born in the very insignificant little town of Frassinocasa in Veneto and came to Rome as a young man to seek my fortune. I was lucky for quite a while, even though – if I must admit it – not always completely honest and god-fearing. Perhaps a similar fate to that which struck the Cenci family might have befallen me one day.

The good fortune – and the misfortune – of my life was that I made friends with Michel, a man utterly apart from the common herd, so much *more* than the common herd. No one could make flowers, fruit or skin come to life on the canvas as he could. No one could come into a gloomy tavern and fill it with *life* as he could.

I admit it: he grew to be more than a friend. He was the one who gave substance to my life, the meaning I should have sought elsewhere – may our Blessed Mother intercede for me – yet I was happy as long as it lasted.

He *saw* me. Yes, he used me as a model. He took my round, strong, young limbs and gave them to John the Baptist or Isaac on the sacrificial altar. It was splendid and fearful: while he held me with his gaze as in a vice, we were no longer friends. He was a conquerer, his brush was exactly like a whip; he swung it with brief commands and I pushed away the tiredness in my legs, forced my mind to ignore the pain in my back, enjoyed the trembling heat of the room on my naked skin, the skin he would have torn from me if the picture had demanded it, so much the more as it was resurrected shining and moist on the canvas, like a miracle. My skin.

And afterwards, out we went into the streets, to the inns and the taverns. He could sing, fence and fight with bare knuckles.

So it was that he could lead a young man into gaol with his drinking and his readiness to pick a fight.

But I was still rather young and inquisitive, and I went on nourishing a passion: I wanted to *know*. Mathematics and astronomy had always been my greatest interests, something del Monte had obviously snapped up. In me he saw a person who could keep him in touch with the sciences that interested him most: alchemy, astronomy and medicine. That was why he sent me to Padua.

If that was the only reason. To send me *away* from Rome, from Michel, from the long hours in front of the canvases, and away from the rumbustious times in the inns, would have been just as much reason. It was an exile, a great man's plan or chance whim that I could not withstand. Del Monte had too many means of crushing the will of others.

Worse fates could have befallen me, I was well aware of that.

I missed Rome, I missed Michel; the thought of him was like a low singing tone I heard every waking hour of the day, it was always with me. All the same, I had many happy days in Padua. I spent a great deal of time in the botanical gardens, eagerly engaged in studying the various herbs and discovering what kind of healing properties they could have. There was learning to be had here: of the names of plants, their habitat, what parts were most valuable and, not least, their effect on the body.

But my real interest was in astronomy. I was not especially driven by the urge to interpret the movements of the stars by casting horoscopes, but I quite simply wanted to *understand* more than other people, to be the one who *knew*. Undoubtedly it is this kind of arrogance that drives many scientists.

As some few will know, many years ago an obscure and confused book was published by a certain Canon Koppernigk, or Copernicus, on the furthest fringes of Catholic Christendom, somewhere beside the Mare Balticum. The title of the book was *De Revolutionibus,* and it seeks in all its hazy incomprehensibility to carry out the calculations of the movements of the heavenly bodies on a completely new basis, namely the literally revolutionary idea that the movement of the fixed stars is not real but only apparent. This remarkable phenomenon is claimed to be due to the fact that *the Earth itself* turns on its own axis. As if this were not mad enough, Copernicus designates *the Sun* as the midpoint of the Universe and reduces the Earth to one planet among several, which in its turn describes orbits around an imaginary point in the vicinity of the Sun!

If one is to take this seriously, then one has to accept that it conflicts with the Lord's own words as Genesis renders them – not to speak of the fact that it is against the teachings of antiquity and the church fathers – and ordinary, simple human common sense. Perhaps that was the very reason for the idea provoking me so much. Why should not the universe be as incomprehensible as Beatrice Cenci's death?

Now, there is much to indicate that Canon Copernicus pictured this as a purely geometric construction, a foundation for more exact calculations of ascensions, conjunctions, eclipses and other phenomena in the vault of heaven. He did in fact carry out such calculations and published new tables which were put into use to the satisfaction of everyone, not least those brave men who in our days sail over all the seas and constantly need to determine their position.

So far so good. No one denied me the right to make calculations according to this model. But already, at the beginning of my studies, another book fell into my hands, written by a young teacher in the royal Steiermark, entitled *Mysterium Cosmographicum*. This not only takes it for granted that the Sun is at the centre and the Earth is one of the planets but maintains that this apparently heretical idea, in reality, is a work of God, full of heavenly harmony!

I was a young man. My life had been unsettled, and this generated a deep longing in me for order and harmony, but like the majority of young men I was curious and impressionable. So when a man a mere few years older than myself came along with an idea so overwhelming and at the same time so *beautiful* it was bound to appeal to me.

This is not the place for a thorough examination of Copernicus's ideas. Let me just say briefly that in reckoning up the Earth he obtains planets that are six in number and that he strives for perfect harmony by demonstrating that in each of the spaces between the presumed courses of these planets around the Sun can be inscribed one of the five perfect polyhedra, that is to say the five platonic bodies: tetrahedron, cube, octahedron, dodecahedron and, finally, the icosahedron itself with its twenty faces.

Even while I sit here, a grown man filled with remorse and contrition, and write this account, I am – may the Mother of God pardon me – almost stunned by the beauty of this idea. There exist five and only five perfect polyhedra; thus has it been since the creation of the Earth and so will it continue until the Day of Judgement – no human powers, no brilliant notion, not the solemn command of the greatest prince can change that. It is as if we can see a faint reflection of perfection itself in God's creative power in this simple Euclidean fact. Five bodies can be constructed, five and only five: tetrahedron cubes, octahedron, dodecahedron, icosahedron. Then imagine being able to raise one's eyes to God's own heaven and *find the same five perfections again there!* The conception is so temptingly lovely, so apparently luminous with holiness, that it is impossible not to be lured by it.

And I allowed myself to be lured.

Kepler professed the Lutheran heresy and denied the Sacred Throne of St Peter. My urge to oppose was possibly so great that this gave his teaching an extra allure for me.

I threw myself upon the *Mysterium Cosmographicum.* The book became an obsession with me. It might have been that Kepler's bold ideas were a kind of substitute for he whom I missed in Rome – I do not hesitate to call the book an idol which led my thoughts into new paths. I read, thought, calculated, observed – indeed, I made plans to ask del Monte to pay for a journey to Graz so I could meet Kepler in person. It cannot be denied that in my youthful arrogance I dreamed of a collabor-

ation with him, a mutual effort that would supply the absolute
validity of the great, beautiful and extremely perilous idea he
demonstrated so temptingly.

For he had only *shown* it proved it he had not, as far as I
understood his work. There were simplifications, adjustments
and plain errors in the immensely complicated calculations;
indeed, although the man was older than I was, I soon discovered
that he had not come so far as I in the understanding of the mysteries of mathematics. It was the *idea* that had struck him, like a
flash of lightning, the certainty that the perfection of geometry is
a revelation of God, that it is a part of God's being from eternity
to eternity. It was in order to prove this idea of his that he had
seized upon the unfortunate notion of the Sun at the centre; not
as a practical model for calculations; no, surely as an expression
of the pure and manifest truth.

There was *one* person at the university with whom I could
share my thoughts. For del Monte had another protégé there.
Through the Grand Duke of Tuscany he had arranged that a man
from Pisa, a few years older than I, should obtain a chair in mathematics at Padua. This talented man seemed to be as much a
mechanic as a scientist. He set competent artisans to making pen-
dulums, metronomes and weights, with which he carried out
his experiments. Unfortunately, he happened to be a pretty
unpleasant person and extremely hard on his students. So I must
admit that I did not seek the advice of this professor as much as
del Monte assumed I did.

The man – whose name was Galileo – was absolutely orthodox in his teaching, but he was one of the first to have read the *Mysterium* and appreciate the ideas it contained. There were two things in particular I disliked about him. One of them was that in his teaching he scornfully repudiated Copernicus by employing precisely such arguments which, in his conversations with me, he elegantly pulled to pieces; for instance, that the Earth would be bound to fall apart if it was exposed to the kind of moving forces that the theory demanded.

The other was a feeling that he did not want to come out with everything he knew, that he would rather question *me* to see what I had understood and mastered for myself – that he did not regard knowledge as a common source of understanding and vision but as private property. Perhaps these two things were connected, I thought, perhaps this Professor Galileo just dishes out the old cosmology to ignorant fools while in secret he works on a dazzlingly new and convincing book, which will undeniably make him the greatest astronomer in the world.

Well, such may be the thoughts of an ambitious young man eager for knowledge, such as I then was. However it was, my relationship with the professor never became close; I mostly worked on by myself. Then I soon discovered something else: that the whole of our proud astronomical science rests on flimsy foundations. The observations were simply too divergent, contradictory and inexact for any certain conclusions to be drawn from them. They contained divergences of half a moon's diameter or more, whether they were caused by cross-eyed observers, mediocre instruments or errors in transcripts during the copying of manuscripts.

I also knew, as did everyone with an interest in astronomy, that a man existed who mastered a hitherto unknown quantity of exact measurements, undertaken with almost exaggerated pedantry over many years, with the largest and most correct quadrants and sextants it was possible to make and guarded with such greed they might have been pearls and precious stones.

Observations. Del Monte had allowed me to hear Borromeo's objections on good grounds. I realized that my employer the cardinal as well found himself drawn in two directions by these two unruly quantities: Faith, which is absolute just because it cannot be proved; and cognition, which is insufficient because it can always be shaken by new measurements, new authentication.

But the great observer, whose name was Tycho, was a Lutheran and thus pretty insane. He was a nobleman in the King of Denmark's chilly and windswept little realm, but he became so impossible that he had to pack up his treasure chest of observations and move to the imperial court of Prague. Indeed, I noted with interest that even His Catholic Majesty the Emperor was not ashamed of taking a heretic into his service, if the apostate was clever enough.

It was chiefly the matter of Mars's capricious course across the vault of heaven. With new and more correct observations it would be possible to calculate whether Kepler's model was more accurate than that of the esteemed Ptolemy, from whom men learned of the stars and who the church fathers have acclaimed for centuries with the deepest respect, whose model has the

Earth standing totally firm under the feet of human beings.

I had finished my preparations for my journey to Graz when the news reached me; news which at that time filled me with anger and despair. Archduke Ferdinand was far more interested in defending the pure teaching than his superior, the Emperor. The severe archduke brought order on his own initiative. He quite simply commanded that all who held to the Lutheran error were to be whipped out of Steiermark. Including Kepler the astronomer.

My journey would thus be in vain, so I gave it up. Today I can see this was very advantageous for the salvation of my soul, but at the time it led to an internal rage against all popes, emperors and dukes. What I did not know but which was told me later in Padua was that Kepler, forced into exile, travelled to Prague in order to meet none other than Tycho, his Danish colleague with the invaluable observations.

There he calculated the course of Mars, which agreed with his theory.

This course of action was immediately interpreted by heretics as the will of God. They said that the good Ferdinand did act in accordance with God's plan for the world when he drove out the Lutherans, but not in the way he himself believed, that it would please God to be quit of the heretics. No, the Lord's wisdom is more inscrutable than human beings can fathom: the exile order forced Kepler into going to Prague, the only place where he could get hold of the observations he needed in order to prove his theory.

Others would probably say that it was rather the Devil himself who put the heretics together in the Emperor's city. And I must crave pardon for the whole of this long *digressio*.

The admittedly somewhat naïve Cardinal Borromeo was right on one point. This is a fact of life: that human observation and divine revealed truth often conflict with each other. There is nothing remarkable in this if one just remembers that the Devil does in fact exist. For it is the quotidien, the senses, the banalities, the familiar and tangible things which are the particular domain of the Devil. He it is who slips his transforming glass between the observer and the observed, he who distorts and confuses what man believes to be the pure unadulterated truth.

That was why Michel's method was dubious. Just like Kepler when he met the mad Dane in Prague, my friend the painter placed complete faith in what he *saw* with his defective human gaze. He did not perceive that the truth comes *from* God and *down to* the human being and cannot be assembled with his wretched, faulty and devil-possessed senses alone.

Of course it was a great sin to use a fallen woman as a model for Catherine. But Merisi's indecent choice of models was, seen from the natural philosophical viewpoint, merely a more far-reaching consequence of his all too fundamental belief in himself.

VII

I went to Padua in the summer of AD 1599 and did not return before a year had passed. I thought I was coming back to my friend Michel, the young, talented and quarrelsome painter. But the man I met in Rome was the mundane artist Caravaggio – indeed, some went so far as to address him as *egregius in Urbe pictor.* * Just one or two even thought my friend could be compared with his great namesake Michelangelo Buonarrotti, but this view was regarded as extreme and greatly exaggerated.

I had looked forward to acting as his model again. I have to admit that this was a kind of longing that lived its own life in my body, while my mind was well pleased to frolic with the mysteries of the starry sky. But Michel no longer needed me in that way. He painted new pictures, he had new models – in particular an elderly but still handsome man almost twice his age, with a high forehead and full beard.

I think I understood him. He was on the way to something new; he wanted to paint *other* pictures. But, needless to say, my pride was hurt, and I often asked myself whether during the course of that year I had deteriorated so much that there was no longer any pleasure to be found in my lithe limbs and smooth skin. At the same time I realized that Michel had gone *beyond* pleasure, beyond the beautiful and attractive.

Michel's explosive fame, a veritable *succès de scandale*, resulted from the pictures he painted for a transverse chapel in S. Luigi, the French church in Rome. The work was originally to have been executed by a boring, easy-going and well-regarded master, the well-born *cavaliere* Guiseppe d'Arpino. His dry and dull paintings of the prophets and the Blessed Matthew's journey

---

* The chosen painter of the City. (Editor's note)

to Ethiopa in fact still adorn the roof vault of the chapel.

Michel's pictures also depict the Blessed Matthew. The first two show how the evangelist receives his calling as a disciple – and his martyrdom. Both are magnificent works of art. Michel is working here with the strong, clear light no one can match him for, even though many consider he exaggerates the contrast between light and dark.

The everyday scene showing the customs officers round the table could have been drawn from a tavern in the neighbourhood. The men are counting money and chatting lazily. And then suddenly Christ himself stands in the doorway, pointing, and with him the light of grace shines into the semi-darkness surrounding the men.

Matthew's face reflects not so much the sanctity of the moment as pure, sheer human amazement; his lips part in a breathless 'Me?' which can virtually be *heard* under the vault of the chapel.

This first picture is painted exceptionally, strikingly well. But the second one – the martyrdom of the evangelist – is the work of a true master. Here Michel's new, elderly friend is the model for Matthew. The artist was already renowned for his ability to imitate nature, right down to rotten patches on apples and light falling through glass vases – but now he sees *through* nature, to that *something* that lies beyond. He feels both joy and pain and paints them together. The body of the executioner is beautiful, well built, harmonious; the light falls upon it – his beauty both denies and emphasizes his cruelty as he seizes the prone apostle's wrist in order to hold him steady as he thrusts the sword into him. Matthew himself, on the other hand, looks past earthly death. He pays no attention to the sword, he does not even look at the executioner – his gaze is directed upwards, at the angel who is coming to present him with the palm of salvation. The circle is complete, now it is the one-time customs officer who stretches out his hand. He does not question any more – he *knows;* composed as he confronts his execution, he gives himself up to the mystery of martyrdom.

But not all go to their death as saints. Michel also knew Beatrice Cenci's horror as she stood there deserted by God and man. And he has painted that horror, recreated it, it shines in the faces and bodies of the people around the Blessed Matthew, the terror that freezes everything, makes time itself stop in the long moment before the murderer plunges the already naked blade into him.

In the background, outside the drama, a sympathetic face looks on; it is Michel's own, participating, pitying, and unable to intervene, as he had been at the Ponte Sant'Angelo.

Yes, that is how he unfolded the two poles in Matthew's life: so that everyone could *step into* it: Christ the Bearer of Light and the executioner with the sword.

But the third picture, which he did not paint until a year or two later, is the best. It presents Matthew and the angel who guides him with the writing of the gospel. Michel painted the holy man as a peasant from the Campagna, with filthy bare feet, without a halo, without dignity, just animatedly engaged in his divine calling. The angel leads his hand over the paper, not to suggest that the holy man could not write, as a few idiots have accused the painter of doing, but to *show* that the Word came from God.

This was himself too, even though he never chose to give his own features to the face of a saint but used his model. Michel was a drunken whoremonger and trouble-making brawler. But I cannot explain the beauty in his paintings in any other way than to say that occasionally, in his wondrous mercy, the Lord grasped his brush – may the Blessed Mother forgive me if I am wrong.

This third picture – in all its splendour – was one of the steps that led to the catastrophe on the Campo Marzio. It was first exhibited at a great Whitsun mass in the year of Our Lord 1602, when many of the cardinals were present, among them the unfortunate Borromeo. Some cried out in disgust. Others, who themselves saw nothing objectionable in the picture, grew afraid of not seeming sufficiently pious, and soon the whole of the reverent congregation hastened to express displeasure over the dirty feet and missing halo.

The picture was taken down, but not before all those interested had managed to see it.

Michel was obliged to paint a new picture with no extra payment. This, too, was a good painting, in which the saint's face in particular simultaneously expresses both despair over the impossible task of finding words for the incomprehensible – and certainty that the angel will help.

The new picture was allowed to hang, but it was a humiliation, a wound in Michel's tortured mind.

No, no. Again I am going much too fast with my account. The first two pictures had already caused a sensation such as no painter had achieved in Rome for many years. It was an anniversary year, the city was full of pilgrims, many from France. Naturally the French visitors sought out their own church. The Romans too streamed to S. Luigi to see, to compare Caravaggio's vivid, suffering people with d'Arpino's flat puppet figures.

The pictures were quite simply too good. A dispute with the academy was inevitable. Old Zuccari, head of the academy, came himself, peered short-sightedly at the pictures and said condescendingly, 'What's so exciting about this?' There was absolutely nothing new in Michel's pictures; they were rather a pale imitation of Giorgione the Venetian, Zuccari concluded firmly, shrugged his shoulders and left.

I have often thought that this little episode was the turning point for Michel, this stupid insult from an insignificent man whom fate had placed in an important position. Michel, who could not endure comparisons with others, who would not admit he had any masters, he was told that he was nothing but a subordinate copyist!

From then on his bodily humours were in severe imbalance. He painted better and better, it is true, but his behaviour grew worse and worse. More and more gall flowed in him, both the black kind, which produces melancholy, and particularly the yellow, the chief component of choler. He got into more fights, even on the open street, and he refused to talk to people he considered below his own rank and dignity. Soon he would even leave our benefactor del Monte.

If the painter no longer needed my help as a model, we remained friends, not to say carousing companions. The hours spent with him were still experience apart from the everyday, festive times that brought joy to my otherwise simple life. One blazing hot summer evening, just after I had come back from Padua, Michel, Onorio Longhi and I walked together across the Piazza Navona. The sun had dropped behind the Gianicolo but the heat still lay in the cobbles; it crept up through our soles and made our feet swell. Then we met a harmless little artist, who unfortunately for him was a pupil of Zuccari, head of the academy.

Michel stopped, his hand shot out and grabbed him by the collar.

'Giorgione?' was all he said.

Of course, the poor wretch had no responsibility for his master's absurd opinions. He tried to shake his head or shrug his shoulders, but Michel hit him in the face without letting go of him. The budding painter howled like a fox held by the tail.

The square was emptying, but there were still a lot of people about. Unfortunately one of them was a sergeant of the guard at Castel Sant'Angelo. He drew his sword and ordered Michel to stop.

The painter's small, compact body was quicker and more supple than it looked. In one movement Michel let go of his victim, turned, drew his own sword and struck the sergeant violently on the hand.

Longhi and I threw ourselves at Michel and held him. Then we took him between us and dragged him the few steps over to the Palazzo Madama, sweating and cursing in the heat, with Michel furiously screaming at us to let go of him so he could make short work of both the guard-devil and that cocksucker of a paint-slosher.

Del Monte restored order, how I do not know. But clearly he must have doled out some unusually sizeable bribes.

<u>VIII</u>

Before I went back to Padua that autumn, two more things occurred.

The first was idiotic beyond compare. We were at an inn not far from Trinità dei Monte, a place we visited merely because the landlord had the good sense to get his white wine from the hills near Frascati.

I said before that Michel's mouth betrayed sensuality. Oh, I can still see him sitting in the inn with his *bruschetta,* that little dish as simple as it is perfect: toasted bread dipped in oil generously spiced with garlic. He bites into the crisp crusty bread with pleasure, lets his lips suck in the soft virgin oil so not a drop escapes, while his tongue glides over the surface of the bread to take in the strong, ecstatic taste of garlic.

He eats, smiles, drinks, talks. He drinks white wine and then grappa. His figure draws all eyes to him, he is a king sitting there, and people notice. But the handsome black suit he was given by del Monte (and is immensely proud of) is soiled and worn to threads. A lad of a trainee waiter sees this, says something or other in the doorway about expensive habits and a shabby good-for-nothing or some such.

Some think the Devil can become flesh as easily as the Lord can. I have never myself seen the Evil One appear openly in his own base person, praised be our Blessed Mother. But unfortunately I have all too often seen him take up residence in a human being, so often that I really believe this is his preferred way of manifesting himself. And that can be bad enough.

In short, the Devil himself or one of his countless assistants took possession of Michel as soon as he heard the boy's remark. He leaps up to throw himself at him, undoubtedly to throttle him with his bare hands, since he does not take the time to find his sword. Chairs and tables crash, food and wine gushes out. The boy flees for his life into the kitchen.

Onorio Longhi and I hurl ourselves at Michel and by our mutual strength manage to restrain both him and the devil by forcing him to the floor. Somehow or other we get him outside, with the landlord's threats of police and demands for restitution as an accompaniment.

We drag the painter away, bellowing like a mad bull. He wants us to lie in wait outside the inn and beat up the wretched apprentice as soon as he comes out. Onorio Longhi and I can think of no other option but to pour grappa into him until he lies senseless and we can carry him back to the Palazzo Madama.

A few days later a messenger called at the Madama. He had been sent by the chief treasurer of the finances of the Holy See, one of His Holiness's closest colleagues and among the most powerful men in Rome. Again *I* was the one who had to accompany my friend, this time not to scrabble drunkenly around on dirty tavern floors but to an audience with the chief treasurer at his offices on the Quirinal Hill.

Del Monte forked out grudgingly for a new silk suit. There were whispers around town that the lord of the Palazzo Madama was no longer so flush with money, that he lived too extravagantly, that his friend and employer the Grand Duke of Tuscany no longer wished to pay him so open-handedly for the services the cardinal rendered the Grand Duchy at the papal court. But Michel remained in his service.

The well-trusted chief treasurer of our Holy Father was a lean elderly man, with a pale face and brown liver spots on his neck and cheeks. In short, he looked like a man for whom it was high time to start thinking about his salvation.

Precisely because of that, perhaps, he showed himself to be a very effectual man who knew what he wanted. He had a banker with him in order to set up a contract with Michel and pay out an advance. It turned out that the treasurer had purchased a side chapel in Sta Maria del Popolo itself, which he wished to have adorned with pictures in honour of God.

He wanted one picture depicting Peter and one of Paul – a man in his position could hardly do less. He may have nourished the hope that a *little* honour would come his way as well, when he had gone and the paintings were left, provided they were glorious pictures that people would remember and talk about. That is the human way of thinking. The Lord looks mercifully upon such innocent vanity.

And his advance was decent enough. At a nod from the treasurer his banker counted out every single coin. Michel carelessly let them fall into his purse. Afterwards we celebrated the advance and consecrated the new silk suit in the most thorough manner.

IX

That spring the Tiber broke its banks.

This happens regularly, and the Jewish quarter always suffers most. In the hollow east of the Ponte Sisto the foaming water regularly finds an outlet; it pours down through the streets and pushes its way into all the houses, frightening old people, carrying away children, if their mothers, running out into the street shrieking, do not manage to pull them to safety.

In truth, no one can be safe from these wild spring floods. There are palaces and noble houses right down on the banks of the Tiber where the water can penetrate, and old people tell how once the flood was so violent that an empty boat was washed the whole way along the Via Condotti and stranded on the square below Trinità del Monti, believe it who will.

But it is always worst for the Jews. It is natural for them to be allotted land in this district, which is so low-lying that it must once have been a swamp. But it is my impression that these people are industrious and hard-working, and they pay their extra taxes for our carnival and races along the Corso without complaining very much. It is a sad thing to have such a terrible sin as the death of Jesus weighing them down, but if they convert they may well find mercy and forgiveness even for this. And then they can move away from the narrow streets beside the bend in the river near Tiber Island.

That spring the floods were particularly bad. All the bridges along the banks were torn away, several palaces had their ground-floor frescoes ruined, three Jews and a fourth person were drowned.

It was an ill omen, an ominous start to the year. As will be understood, it was with misgivings that I made my way back to Padua.

Del Monte had cut down my subsistence and I could have cancelled my journey, I could have stayed with Michel. But the painter had changed – and I, I was too immersed in my work. The dream of the five perfect bodies had not left me. I had relinquished the hope of meeting Kepler personally, but I could not forget his ideas and worked on quietly with calculations of the heliocentric universe. Incidentally, I did not hide the nature of my work from my colleagues; I described the whole thing as a purely philosophical system from which one could make the necessary astronomical calculations with greater precision than formerly.

All the same, I must say that a few of the university professors regarded my work with the utmost mistrust. There was no likelihood that the young Galileo, whom I have mentioned before, would support me in the presence of the faculty. But privately he was as eager as ever to discuss Kepler.

I cannot deny that this made me uneasy, both Galileo's apparent duplicity and the opposition of the powerful elders. But in my youthful impetuosity I interpreted the attitude of these men to be ruled by their wish to defend their own position. The careful interpretation of Ptolemy they took pains to impart to us students was, of course, the very basis of their position. If Kepler's ideas were to prevail, large areas of their teaching would crash to the ground. They would be obliged to revise their books from scratch and write new lectures. They would also be forced to learn proper mathematics – something which, to be honest, would be an extremely difficult task for them at their advanced age.

In short, without properly realizing it, I compared myself to my friend from Caravaggio. Where *he* made his exact observations of human beings in light and shade and painted them as they were, no matter whether they were to depict saints or sinners, to the disgust of many, I made *my* observations of the vault of heaven and interpreted the objections of my superiors as anxiety and envy, without ever seriously considering that they were worried about the salvation of my soul in a fatherly way and wanted to lead me away from a heretical route.

Then an episode occurred that bewildered me. I had a visit in Padua from a man who invited me out for a walk in the Orto Botanico. At first he did not reveal his errand but talked absent-mindedly about the various plants in the garden, especially the magnificent *Archangelica* or angelica from the high north, which through its very name revealed its powerful and healing qualities and had been coaxed to grow successfully only with great difficulty, as if it missed the poor soil and cool regions where it originally grew and therefore did not thrive in the rich earth and profuse sunshine of Padua.

However, my visitor was not only well informed on medicine, he was also an astronomer. And not merely that. He held a high position in the Society of Jesus itself, those deeply learned and powerful guardians of the purity of the Faith under the special protection of His Holiness. I shall call him Pater T. After having assured himself that our conversation in the garden was out of earshot of anyone, he revealed the true motive for his visit.

He had, he said slowly, come to discuss my work on Kepler and his system.

It must be easy to imagine how I felt, how my courage and my strength seemed to drain out of me, leaving a pathetic figure of withered straw.

I had heard about what happened on the Campo de'Fiori that February day when the unfortunate man from Nola was burned. Now I well knew that Giordano's heresy encompassed far more than his astronomical delusions.

All the same, Death comes to us all. It can take the form of bubonic plague that turns a human being into a rotten sack of pus and matter, of leprosy that gnaws away the limbs one by one, of crazed, raging warriors who cut down, beat, crush and burn, or of the executioner's chilling axe blade that parts the head from

the body. But to be bound to the stake, in the middle of the waiting pile of wood, to stand as a living pillar of fire for long minutes . . . perhaps that is only a small foretaste of Hell's eternal
torments. Certainly one should think much more of the salvation
of one's soul through all eternity than of the insignificant final
minutes of the fate of the earthly shell. All the same, in my childhood I had often tried to stand close to a fire for as long as I
could, up to the moment when I felt how the heat began to eat
into my skin and I *had* to drag myself away.

A person bound to the stake could not drag himself away.

In short, I was scared to death when the Jesuit father
broached the topic of Kepler. I was instantly struck by passionate
remorse – those ideas I had conceived, those calculations I had
been so proud of. How infinitely idiotic it was to live in such an
arrogant fantasy world, outside the real one, a world which with
one blow could bring so much sorrow and suffering on both
myself and people close to me!

My wonderment and terror when Pater T. came out with his
purpose is surely understandable: he bade me earnestly go on
working with the idea of the Sun as the centre of the universe and
the Earth as an insignificant little planet, on a par with Mars and
Venus.

At first I thought it was a trap, to lure me into making my
heresy so plain that there was no way back. But at once I realized this thought was as absurd as it was arrogant: why should
the mighty Society of Jesus take such pains to dispose of a little
student in Padua?

Pater T. noticed my confusion and clarified his words in more detail. The Society, as I knew, preached the Gospel in many parts of our globe, following the example of the good Francis Xavier on his endless journeys to fruitful Brazil, strange India, the savage tribes of Malacca and, not least, the great and powerful Japanese Empire.

Of course I knew this. But did it have to do with the Sun's place in the universe?

Well, it concerned astronomical tables and calculations, said Pater T. Not only was it important that every table dealing with the heights of the Sun and stars should be accurate as far as ever possible when men were navigating in distant and unknown waters, but it had been found to have a wonderfully powerful effect on the furthering of the Faith when the Society's envoys could foretell marvellous manifestations in the heavens – in particular, eclipses of the Sun and Moon. However, these predictions had to be correct to be of any value. And the old tables were unreliable in those distant regions – there were errors of hours, indeed, days!

Was it not true, he asked me, that the new system gave better and more reliable results?

I had to admit there was much to indicate this but that there was still an immense amount of work to do.

'You must do that work, my son!' said Pater T.

I hesitated to answer, and he understood.

'You are afraid this is a heretical idea,' he said. 'My son, you must not concern yourself too much with the position of the Sun or the Earth in the heavens. The Sun is precisely where the Lord in his immeasurable mercy has placed it. Our miserable human understanding was not made in order to penetrate to the depths of such mysteries. Provide the Society with the figures we have need of, that is a task pleasing to God.'

There I stood, like a child between two flocks of wild beasts: *astronomers* who found my work ungodly, *priests* who considered it to offer significant knowledge.

I continued to work, always with that feeling in my body, an unease, as if I was fencing with unprotected flanks, a naked point where mishap could strike me with a sudden deadly cut. I observed, calculated, compared. Now and then I talked to Professor Galileo, who probably felt the same unease, since he went on with his teaching on the old system as enthusiastically as ever. Our conversations did not get me much further; I had the feeling that I had to pass on ten of my calculations to him before he unwillingly relinquished one of his.

But, as the Jesuit had said, the new calculations gave more accurate results on many points, although not always. I vacillated, I doubted; I cast my horoscope with a secret fear of finding omens of burning at the stake, of misfortune and damnation.

Then came the Sign from Heaven.

<u>X</u>

None can match painters in slandering each other. They are like shrewish women who reply, when questioned about their neighbour's housekeeping, 'Well, of course it is all well and good in some ways, but . . .' and then vent their spleen in no uncertain manner. The exceptions are those who share a studio or work in the same style, but they praise each other in the same immoderate way, so *that*, too, is irritating to hear. Unfortunately I have to admit that in this respect Michel was one of the worst offenders, perhaps the very worst – *deterius in Urbe obtrectator!**

This made for my friend even more enemies than all his intemperance, brawling and financial dealings put together. The man's wild and uncontrollable fury was shown by his inability to forget Zuccari's absurd comparison of him with Giorgione. He let fly at his opponents, not, mark you, at Zuccari in person but at that master's friends and pupils.

Added to that was the brawl with that witless son of a whore Mao Salini, who was to cause so much trouble for Michel.

I was not in Rome when the first skirmishes took place, but unfortunately I am not sure that would have helped. I could have diverted, smoothed over, flattered – but I could have been dragged into the madness as well. However it all was, Michel was left more and more to his friend Onorio Longhi, the architect, a man with an wild and irrepressible nature equal to his own.

The painter Mao Salini could certainly not be called an attractive personality. He was a tall, thin man with a narrow face and long, rather unkempt hair. Several of his teeth were missing, and he wore coarse, threadbare, woollen clothes. Yet he obvi-

---

* The worst slanderer in town. (Editor's note)

ously wanted to give the impression of a person of consequence. He lived with his wife – to whom, unfortunately, passing reference will be made later in this account – in a grubby little room where he also painted his pictures. He took pride in producing profane paintings without animals or people, known as *nature morte*.

Such pictures were in fashion and thus easier to sell by painters who did not have ecclesiastical commissions or a wealthy protector. This was a genre Michel too had practised in his youth, and for a while Mao Salini had pestered Michel into accepting him as a pupil, an arrangement bound to be short-lived. Salini more than hinted publicly that the hostility between the two arose because the master from Caravaggio regarded him, Salini, as a dangerous competitor, one who had outclassed him in this curious craft, the painting of fruits, flowers, vases and other objects pertaining to daily life.

Michel's *nature morte* was painted with terrifying expertise. Yes, I say terrifying, because there was something bewitched about the canvases. It was not only that the colour was uncannily lifelike down to the minutest degree, but the viewer was almost irresistibly tempted to stretch out his hand to touch these grapes, apples and oranges. They were painted so that the variation in the surface of every single fruit could be almost felt: the smooth moistness of the grapes, the dry, slightly wrinkled skin of the apple, the coarse patterning of the orange. One caught oneself thinking that there was something offensive about this virtuosity, as if the artist had dared to enter into competition with the Creator.

Everyone with the sight of only half an eye could see the vast difference between Michel's works and the crude 'fruits' Salini had painted – in which the discoloration was not due to the delicate recreation of a rotten patch in all its distasteful brown sponginess but to the artist's lack of talent for mixing the correct shade.

I was informed that Michel had been arrested by the police yet again while I was occupied with my own affairs in Padua. He was charged with hunting down Salini, beating him with a stick and bawling him out in the open street for being a goat and a cuckold.

Since I was well acquainted with my friend, I did not for a moment doubt the accuracy of the charges. But it would not have occurred just because the wretch had put Michel's own work into the shade; it was because Salini was a miserable imitator and plagiarist who brought shame on his exemplar.

Miserable imitator and plagiarist, certainly. But not without connections. Mao Salini knew Ranuccio Tomassoni.

Mao may well have been a pasty-faced coward, but Ranuccio came from a family who lived by the sword.

XI

It is imposssible to understand Michel without realizing that he *had* to make enemies. Indeed, it might seem as if he sought out the very people who would cause him most trouble and engaged in a methodical campaign of fault-finding against them. The worst thing he could have done was to pick a quarrel with the painter Baglione.

I have mentioned the paintings of St Matthew in S. Luigi, the ones that brought my friend fame. But the pictures of St Peter and St Paul that he painted for the old treasurer of Sta Maria del Popolo created an even greater stir, in addition to the rumours circulating about his behaviour.

It was the horse in particular. Michel painted the conversion of St Paul with an enormous *horse* that captured the viewer's gaze, as if on his way to Damascus the apostle had just fallen off his horse, was lying flat on the ground, blinded by a light from the sky, while the gigantic animal, which takes up three-quarters of the canvas, threatens to trample on him.

From the brush of a slapdash artist this would have had a tasteless and absurd effect. After all, it is *God* who knocks the apostle to the ground – is it the artist's intention to represent God in the figure of a horse? But the master from Caravaggio fills the solid body of the horse with such overpowering force that the viewer himself is crushed to the earth. It is a preposterous and wonderful painting, in which the massive, surging reality observed by the artist is imbued with something *Else*. It is a miracle that happens: the painter observes and renders the flesh, the substance, in such a way that it is pervaded by spirit. I have no better word for this spirituality, this Other than Holiness.

Then there was the *Crucifixion of St Peter*, which I still visualize every time I walk up to the Gianicolo. It captures the moment when the cross with the saint upon it is turned upside down. Three executioners like stout workmen struggle with the heavy burden, the cross is massive and solid, the apostle himself still a powerful if elderly figure. Perfectly rendered is the blend of defiance, horror and saintly surrender on Peter's face. And, as always with Michel, the viewer is drawn into the picture, to be present and to commiserate.

When you study this painting, its lines inevitably draw your gaze to the rough nail which pierces the apostle's left hand and nails it to the cross beam. The difference between Michel and other, less talented painters is simple: the others *assert* suffering, by painting a distorted face or women with tear-filled eyes wringing their hands.

Michel *paints* the suffering. This is what suffering looks like: a nail through a hand, naked metal through naked flesh. You see, you feel, you have to take hold of your own hand.

Well, I was about to tell of Giovanni Baglione. As Michel was finishing his two pictures in Sta Maria del Popolo, this Baglione, who incidentally is not without talent, received a prestigious assignment from the Society of Jesus. It was the most important commission imaginable in Rome at that time; a picture for the altar in Il Gesù itself, the centre of the Jesuits' works of mercy all around our globe.

Everyone familiar with the situation discerned that this was a challenge, a contest. Michel's pictures were too good, there was no ignoring them. Baglione would have to paint in Michel's new, striking manner, with real people, with sharp light and gloomy shadows. But he must show a quite different respect and humility in the treatment of the motif, so that in future Baglione could get the great ecclesiastical commissions while no one could claim that Michel was being slighted.

But, alas, Baglione set to work with *far* too much respect and humility. He painted a gigantic *Resurrection,* one of the largest canvases ever seen, but a work so bloodless and honey-sweet that it could neither please the Lord nor vex His enemies.

Baglione's picture was a fiasco, everyone could see that, even those who were indignant over Michel's painting style or his temperament and way of life. *The Resurrection* spoke for itself, and the rest should have been silence. But, sadly, Michel was far too corrosively bitter and envious because *he* had not been given that assignment. He did not have the sense to hold his tongue and let Baglione sit there with his fiasco; he had to speak out to anyone who would listen: '*The Resurrection* is a tasteless painting, the worst thing he has done.'

It was at this time that Michel left the Palazzo Madama. I do not rightly know why. It is very probable that del Monte grew tired of intervening with all kinds of official bodies every time Michel was in trouble. But no doubt Michel grew tired of the cardinal as well. I assume the latter continued to ask for paintings of the kind Michel no longer wanted to paint, pictures of beautiful young lads: Cupid, John the Baptist when young, the naked Isaac on the altar under Abraham's raised knife. In short, the kind of pictures he had painted at the time when *I* still shared a tiny thrill of the almost sacramental joy it was to see oil and pigment transformed on canvas into a veritable young firm body.

The painter Baglione is actually no fool. He was well aware

that Michel had a unique talent. Later – after the catastrophe – I heard he had written to a friend: 'Caravaggio is not dedicated to his work. When he has painted for a week or two he devotes himself to amusement for a couple of months, with a big sword at his side and a servant. He swans from one game to another, all too willing to duel or instigate a fight, to the extent that it is difficult to engage in sensible conversation with him.'

Indeed, Giovanni Baglione is basically an amiable, attractive person, if perhaps somewhat vain with his large wig and brocade doublet – and that unfortunate gold necklace. He is certainly not one to fight in the street, insult people or threaten them with the sword. He is a simple Christian who paints with unaffected and confident piety. In truth, with him there are no looming horses or holy men with dirty feet! His pictures are comprehensible and elevating for all – and they bore the life out of the observer. They bore our long-suffering Lord to distraction, I imagine, if He ever takes the slightest interest in all the art painted in His honour.

Now Michel was getting plenty of commissions from the most high-ranking people. He painted a really remarkable picture for a certain marquis, a *Doubting Thomas* which at the time interested me greatly.

The picture shows the precise moment when Thomas, doubting but curious, thrusts his finger into Christ's wound for assurance. At that time I regarded Thomas as an observer, one who was not satisfied with the traditional account. In fact, his doubt was the mark of his nobility – he wanted to experience realities before he accepted the miracle! And Jesus permitted this act. Thus, I considered, faith and knowledge rose into a higher unity, with the explicit sanction of the Lord.

Thomas the observer, whose name signifies 'twin'.

For his part the marquis was completely enthralled by this picture, and immediately commissioned another. Then Merisi for once painted one of his old themes, a *Love Victorious* – with his young servant as the model, incidentally.

This would have been all well and good if it had not been for the fact that the marquis had a brother who was a cardinal. The cardinal was also a patron of art, indeed to such an extent that the brothers engaged in quite a keen contest as to who could acquire the best pictures.

And Baglione was still Michel's leading rival, thought the cardinal, as presumably most Romans saw it. The misfortune occurred when he requested Baglione to paint a *Love Divine*. Naturally Baglione did this gladly, in his customary smooth and attractive style. The cardinal was delighted with the result. He considered he had gained an Amor to match that of his brother and rewarded Baglione with a heavy gold necklace.

Something might imply that the marquis was the real connoisseur in the family.

<u>XII</u>

But Michel's meaningless arrogance had burst all bounds: he could not even endure being compared with others. Old grudges were fed by new jealousies. He was crazy enough to feel that Baglione's award of a gold chain was an insult to Michel himself.

Then he was egged on by that boor Onorio Longhi, who never let an opportunity pass of provoking a brawl, and I had come back from Padua and unfortunately took part in the fray myself.

We went around spreading slanderous rumours about Baglione at all the inns and even brothels in the stretches between the Via della Scrofa and the Tiber. But Onorio and I went too far when we cooked up some really colourful sonnets, which no one could make me declaim now even if the executioner himself tried me with his thumb screws.*

It cut really close to the bone when the lampoons derided the cardinal's magnificent gift in a highly derogatory manner, even casting doubt on the genuine value of the necklace. It might not have been so bad if the poems – if so they can be called – had merely lampooned Baglione, but unfortunately they also roped in Mao Salini's horse-faced wife, noted above, and her stinking and all too gaping crotch.

It can undoubtedly be said of our verses that they had halting feet, but nevertheless they limped their way through the whole of Rome in a few days. They reached Baglione – and Mao Salini.

Baglione might have been man enough to ignore these absurdities. But Mao had not forgotten the thrashing Michel had given him with his stick on the open street. Now he could come forward and demand the restitution of his wife's honour – as if the slut had ever had any. He displayed more cunning here than

---

* One or two examples of the sonnets are transcribed in Dell'Acqua and Cinotti: *Il Caravaggio*, Milan, 1971. An example of their level and tone is one in which Baglione is called Giovanni Coglione (Italian for 'testicle'). (Editor's note)

you would expect of such a half-wit. He collected evidence by getting a miserable sot, a painter by the name of Philippo Trisegni, to write out a couple of poems the wretch had heard recited in a tavern. Apparently he was to be rewarded by a few hours of instruction in painting from Mao – one can just imagine what kind of a dauber he was. These verses – in scrawled copies that certainly did not improve them – were to be the grounds for a charge of libel and slander.

As usual, the city authorities' reaction was as tardy as it was incompetent. Onorio made use of the opportunity to make himself scarce: he went out into the Campagna. But some days later they eventually arrested Michel Angelo, myself – and Philippo Trisegni!

Well, Philippo, that hyena of a paint-splasher, was released a few days later, after he had done his best to slander the rest of us. Michel and I ended up in the town prison on the Capitol. The cells there were somewhat drier than the papal cellars in the Tor di Nona, it is true, but the cockroaches were equally fat and the food exquisitely bad.

The court hearing was Michel's show from beginning to end. I myself was merely an extra; they asked me a couple of brief questions and threw me out. But my friend from Caravaggio spoke so loudly and passionately that I could easily follow the proceedings from where I sat in irons out in the vestibule.

He demanded respect, and the court gave it to him. I do not think this was purely due to the invisible circle of great names that surrounded him: cardinals, bankers, marquises, chief treasurer. It was equally down to his physical presence: the brute strength inherent in the compact, dark figure, that almost imperious naturalness of his, as clear when he painted as when he drank and fought – or spoke.

My friend Michel Angelo Merisi, known as Caravaggio, was a man who could certainly read and write, who owned ten or twelve books but who had never had any formal education apart from his training as a painter. As his learned judges well knew, he was not only involved in a case of defamation, he had been accused of offences against the public order several times. It was true that he had protectors among the most prominent men of the city, but he also associated with whores and panders and decorated his language with various flowers from their mouths. Despite these drawbacks he directed a long and distinctly condescending explanation at the judges, certain they would hear him out with interest.

He spoke of the difference between good and bad painters. He explained that a painter's honour is closely bound up with the work that he does and not with his behaviour as an ordinary citizen. He considered that a good painter's honour as an artist obviously exempts him from guilt in ordinary civil cases – and conversely that bad painters may freely be slandered by the good ones, since their incompetence renders them without honour at the start!

Where Baglione was concerned he declared patronizingly that the man was not entirely lacking in talent but that he was a cautious person, bordering on the contemptible. But he only had this remark to offer regarding Mao Salini: 'It is possible that he amuses himself with splotching something together, but I have never seen a *work* by this Mao.'

All the same, to end with he denied having written the verses, as he arrogantly declared that he did not indulge in that kind of child's play, either in Latin or the vernacular.

The court listened but did not believe him. He was pronounced guilty and sent to prison. The judge found house arrest insufficient in his case – so much the more so because he had previously been sentenced to similar punishment following various brawls and molestations, to absolutely no effect.

So Michel was condemned to the galleys.

XIII

Even the good judge must impose penalties; his goodness resides not in a lack of severity but in the *right* degree of severity, and in finding the mildest penalty he can advise according to the circumstances. For instance, he can see to it that penitent heretics receive an additional sentence of a secular kind and are thus condemned to decapitation instead of the stake.

However it all may be, when it comes to the severity of punishment, for a painter, not least for such an arrogant and egotistical practitioner of his profession as my friend, sentencing to the galleys must be equivalent to capital punishment. One can imagine how those sensitive painter's hands would look after only a few months' drudgery rowing in a naval galley with three tiers of heavy oars. Moreover, very few prisoners survive a sentence of several years; the exhausting grind and meagre provisions slowly wear down even the strongest physique.

Onorio Longhi was sentenced *in absentia,* but he would be let off imprisonment if he could pay damages of 1,000 scudi. Both money and architect soon turned up, and Onorio was able resume his boisterous rounds of second-rate taverns, with his risky companions and dubious lady friends.

I myself was sentenced to a mere year's exile from the city, or, if you will, to continue and complete my studies in Padua, a sentence that fully reflects my own insignificance, although perhaps not my actual share in the crime itself. But it turned out to be a fateful year, for when I returned I was no longer an astronomer – and my intimacy with Michel was gone for ever.

But, as has been seen over and over again in my account, there were plenty of admirers of the art of this pugilistic boozer in the loftiest circles, so that time and again he was rescued from circumstances that would have been fatal for others, and Michel was not destined to end his days in the galleys. The French envoy to the Holy See himself intervened and procured his pardon.

On the face of it, this highly unusual intervention was fairly easy to explain. The ambassador was grateful to Merisi for the pictures in S. Luigi, of which the French people in Rome were mightily proud.

Now time has passed and I have begun to wonder. These confused episodes, these apparently absurd outbreaks of violence and slander must surely form a *pattern*. Even though sin in itself *is* in fact chaos, lack of respect for the divine ordering principle in all things, there should yet be some underlying element that could be grasped, if by no other means than with the aid of God's grace and the intercession of the saints. Or perhaps it is merely my years of preoccupation with the order of the heavens which makes me think so. I have spent a lot of time pondering and trying to find the secret that lies at the centre of all these foolish, confusing happenings.

But I have been unable to find any such centre in Michel's universe, either an Earth or a Sun.

XIV

No, it will not do. I have read through this account and see that it still jumps about far too much. I have not even written about the Sign from heaven that ended my time as an astronomer. May the Holy Virgin help me to gather my thoughts, so my reader does not expire from impatience.

Man proposes, God disposes. The whole enormous clash between old and new, between Ptolemy and Kepler, indeed all our laborious, industrious, fastidious work on improving our calculations of the course of the stars through the firmament and on predicting conjunctions and eclipses, took on an absurdly different appearance when the Lord in His absolute omnipotence caused a completely new star to make its entrance.

This shining *stella nova* that appeared in the sky with no warning whatsoever, brilliant as Venus itself, filled scholars all over the Christian world with fear and wonder. Many interpreted it as an intimation of the Lord's imminent Second Coming – this then must be the same star as the one seen by the shepherds in the field. Others viewed it as a sure sign of wars, plague and earthquake, as if any extra sign was needed for those, which are part of our daily lot!

But in my case I was jerked out of the delusion I had lived with – and for – for so long. I glanced up from my studies of Kepler's calculations, up at the very heavens he sought to describe, and realized that I was on the wrong track. What could my observations and improvements of calculations by a full hour or minute of an arc be worth? The Lord God overthrew every human calculation and model; without the least warning he had set a completely new star in the sky just when it pleased him.

I actually said that to Professor Galileo, for I knew that purely privately he had begun to circulate certain manuscripts that did not perhaps go as far as Kepler but rested on the idea itself: the Sun at the centre. The Professor assured me that he agreed, that the new star seemed to be a sign from the Lord telling us that we must not contest the clear descriptions of the universe in the Bible and in tradition: *There shall be lights in the firmament of heaven to divide the day from the night; and let them be for signs, and for seasons, and for days, and years.*

More clearly it cannot be said. A fortnight later my year of exile was ended, and I travelled straight back to Rome. I obtained, despite my earlier misdemeanours, a modest post as a scribe in the Society of Jesus, where I continue to work, although now in a rather more responsible post.

Here I have kept myself away from temptation and carousing companions.

I embarked on this long account at the injunction of the Curia, but I must admit that it has gradually begun to live its own life, that I have written it just as much for myself, in order to organize all the thoughts that come to me every evening up on the Gianicolo. But where is it leading?

Michel's misfortune was obviously due to several things, which yet are linked. For all these things flow from the one: the painter put himself and his observations first, as the basis for everything. He was a Kepler, a Tycho, a Protestant. And calamity had to strike him.

One thing is his destructive urge to make all those who were not his close friends into his bitter enemies. Ranuccio Tomassoni was obviously thinking of his painter friend's honour when – in the manner in which I heard it – he stormed out of his house and started to revile Michel. All the insults, all the scorn and derision Michel had poured out on his less talented colleagues, Mao Salini's lack of wit, Zuccari's exaggerated vanity, Baglioni's wounded professional pride – all came together in Ranuccio's sword.

If I am convinced that this was the real reason for the fatal encounter, despite all the talk of a wager, a gaming debt and I don't know what else, it is because a number of strange happenings were played out afterwards, which I do not need to go into here. To put it briefly, Baglione was set upon by four painters on his way out of Sta Trinità dei Monti after mass. The painters were friends – or perhaps, rather, young followers – of Michel. The case was officially settled with fines and shelved as a drunken brawl.

It is nothing new for painters to land themselves in fights. But there must have been a reason for the young tearaways to set upon the dignified Baglione. For my part there is no doubt that the budding painters held Baglione directly or indirectly responsible for Caravaggio – as everyone calls him now – having to flee from the city and wanted to show support for their absent master in this heedless manner.

Another cause of the misfortune is Onorio Longhi. The mood of this man can alternate from merry, almost exaggerated cameraderie via a dark and dangerous melancholy to pure evil. He is especially like that when he is in drink, and that he mostly is. Michel should have kept away from such a man, but instead he made the architect his best friend – another example of that urge to paint everything in black and white, to make decisions that in the end damaged himself most of all.

Of course they had been drinking on that ill-fated evening, Ranuccio and his friends as well. The way from word to sword was even shorter than usual. But all the same – if I am to believe what I was told by eye-witnesses – the fire might have died down if Onorio had not blown on it with glee.

My witness is Corporal Paolo, who was with Michel and Onorio. He says that Ranuccio, his brother and two other men were on their way out of the house, when Michel, Onorio and the others came walking by. Michel could not control his tongue, as usual. May the Blessed Mother forgive me, but I feel bound to repeat his words exactly as spoken. He shouted at Ranuccio: 'Has that dauber Salini been sucking your cock lately, Tomassoni? Or perhaps you prefer to use his toothless hag?'

But Ranuccio merely shrugged his shoulders.

'You owe me ten scudi, painter,' he said. 'But everyone knows you can't be relied on in either words or money matters. An IOU from you is as worthless as your ridiculous insults. I suppose I shall have to come and get the money myself if I want it.'

Michel stopped short, slightly uncertain. Then Onorio shouted: 'He insults you, Michel! That blockhead friend of the worst paint dabblers in town allows himself an opinion on *you*! Let us go down to the playing field – let me be your second!'

My witness, Corporal Paolo, swears he tried to stop them, and one of Ranuccio's friends did so too. But now the two of them went on down, pushing and bawling at each other, the whole way to the playing field. There both of them drew their swords.

'For all they that take the sword, shall perish by the sword.'

Innocenzo Promontorio's actual report, by far the fullest of those found, ends here. However, this person wrote another short note on the case. This was – for reasons that will become obvious – written after the other reports, and I therefore choose to place it at the end, where it belongs chronologically. (Editor's note)

The Account of
Onorio Longhi

I WAS ASSIGNED *to travel to Milan in order to take down Onorio Longhi's account of the circumstances relating to the painter Merisi's crime and flight from Rome. This man's statement was so brief that I have simply chosen to give it here in its entirety, exactly as I wrote it down from notes immediately after the conversation. But let me first mention my impression of Longhi the architect: he is just over medium height and powerfully built, approaching forty years old, with coarse features, brown hair of medium length and a somewhat sparse and quite fair beard. At first he spoke slowly but with great conviction; later his words streamed out so fast that it was hard for me to construe it all, and his tone became almost a whine. A man who was sure of his own education and stature but who seemed unstable and appeared almost vain, clad in a suit of rich black velvet that would have seemed far too elegant for his position if it had not been so lamentably shabby.*

I have taken pains to reproduce his extremely unseemly language exactly, even though many of his words weighed heavy on my pen, indeed, to such an extent that I have found it hard to read

*through what I myself have written. I detest breaking the bounds
of seemliness, and obviously I should not have done so here even
if my motive was to report the truth. But I felt it must be the right
thing to do in this case, may God's Blessed Mother aid me with
forgiveness.*

*I began by begging him to give an exact account of the cir-
cumstances attending the murder itself, and to follow this by
explaining himself and how he had evaded justice.**

Politics is a disease.

Or is it a part of man's sinful nature? Can it really be true that
when one group dresses in white another group *must* run
straight to the tailor to order black suits? When some support
papal power others are bound to sacrifice body and soul to the
emperor, when some side with the Spaniards are we others
driven by our demons to work wholeheartedly for the Frenchies'
cause?

I am not sure of anything any more. I only know that 28 May
was a day of disaster.

We were all so happy in January AD 1605. The white smoke
had signalled that Alessandro de Medici of Florence had been
elected, and we looked forward to a new life in the city – with an
end to the influence of the foolish reactionary Spaniards, a time
when folk could hold opinions and voice them without straight-
away running the risk of having their joints broken, their tongue

---

* This is apparently the scribe's own comment, as it is written in the same hand as
the report itself. (Editor's note)

pulled out and their head exhibited on a stake. People poured through the streets shouting: 'France has conquered! Blessed be the French! Long live France! Long live Florence!'

We know what happened. The Pope from Florence died suddenly, and I shall guard myself from opining what he actually died of. The spring was an uneasy time. The city was almost lawless, small gangs ruled the streets. Giovan Franscesco Tomassoni was *caporione* on the Campo Marzio. He and his brothers had set up their own small army in the district. After the winter riots some of their friends who supported the Spaniards were incarcerated at the Capitol, but Giovan Franscesco stormed in with his men, beat up the gaolers and set their friends free.

Those of us friendly towards the French could do little. The Spanish party gained power with the election of His present Holiness. He was enthroned on 28 May, and I shall not disguise the fact that we were not overjoyed at the installation of this Borghese fellow. On that day we drank and wrangled with anyone who looked to be friendly with the Spanish, those we thought were putting on airs, with tall hats, pigtails and black silk stockings. Naturally Michel was arrested, for the umpteenth time.

And was set free again, as usual. Incidentally, he was arrested yet another time – or was it several times? – later that same summer. Oh, Michel, he could provide work for a whole army of policemen!

I think it was something to do with a notary and a woman, an insignificant whore he had used as a model and who would not leave him in peace afterwards. She gave him a lot of trouble.

But that was an entirely different matter. The thing I have to tell you about took place the following year, as you know, on the actual anniversary of the enthronement of Pope Borghese. The city was full of people celebrating the day. A year is a very long time for most. The crowds in the street had forgotten their opposition to the Spaniards and were rejoicing over the fireworks His Holiness had ordered to be let off from Castel Sant'Angelo.

But not everyone had forgotten. That evening there were four of us, Captain Petronio Troppa and Corporal Paolo from Bologna as well as Michel and myself. We had watched the processions the French and Spanish had laid on from their respective churches and all of us agreed, by God, that the French show was the most splendid. We were on our way to the playing field at the Campo Marzio. As we were passing the house of that miserable scoundrel, that Spanish *aficionado*, the fool Ranuccio Tomassoni, we heard voices from inside calling out to Michel to stop.

I myself was not carrying any weapon, neither was Paolo. But the Captain was armed, and Michel himself never went anywhere without his good sword. All of the four men who came out of the house were heavily armed. All the same, Michel could not hold his tongue, any more than all the other times. He yelled at Ranuccio: 'Get down and suck a Spanish cardinal's cock! They have need of some small comfort after their miserable procession!'

I immediately recognized a scarred warrior with whom I had drunk a good many glasses before the damned politics parted us. It was Ranuccio's brother Giovan Franscesco, the one I mentioned just now, who had the troublemakers released. He was about to set upon Michel at once, but Ranuccio held him back.

'I came out to demand my money of you,' he said. 'You still owe me ten scudi from the day I beat you at *pallacorda*. But now it sounds as if you want to pay a bigger debt!'

Michel replied: 'I have never yet lost a game to a Spanish cocksucker and papal arselicker!'

While the two of them wrangled we had arrived at the edge of the playing field. There Ranuccio drew his sword and went for Michel.

'Beg my pardon or fight!' he shouted.

But Michel stood there calmly. 'A man of honour has nothing to gain by fighting with such as you,' he said. 'You had better take care now, Ranuccio! You've lost your wits already, why do you want to lose your head as well?'

Then Ranuccio raised his sword and struck hard, but with the side of his blade, at Michel's head. Our friend Captain Petronio drew his weapon and advanced, as did Giovan Franscesco Tomassoni. Michel clapped his hand to his head and we saw he was bleeding so profusely that the blood ran down his chin and neck. Then he finally drew his sword and attacked Ranuccio.

They were both good swordsmen, Ranuccio Tomassoni heavier and stronger, Michel swifter. The sun was setting behind the Gianicolo Hill. The swords clashed with hard, snapping sounds. We could hear the sound of quick steps on the dry sandy ground. No one said anything, none of us called encouragement or warning, not even Petronio or Giovan Franscesco who stood still with their swords drawn, as if they were seconds and this was a duel of honour.

It was no duel. It was an idiotic, blind struggle, for life or death. But we all saw it. Michel was driven back. He was always a bit slow, met his opponent's thrust at the last moment, so that although he warded off the blow he did not manage to summon his forces for a forward lunge of his own. The blood ran faster and faster from his head wound; it looked as if it hampered his vision, in any case he was losing so much blood that his strength was affected.

Then everything happened at once. Captain Petronio shouted 'Enough!' and stepped forward with raised blade. It was clear he meant to stop them, but before he could reach them Giovan Franscesco was on him and inflicted a great slash on his right shoulder. Petronio screamed, dropped his sword and collapsed. Ranuccio was about to make an attack but was disturbed by what was happening and almost stumbled, so that he was forced to take a couple of unsteady steps backwards.

Michel saw his opening and struck. The sword penetrated deep into Ranuccio's left side, and he fell. It seemed to me he was dead before he struck the ground.

They lay there, the two of them: Petronio uttered short, gasping moans, Ranuccio was bloody and motionless. A number of people had gathered around. We had not noticed them while the fight was proceeding. Some started to call for guards and police. Then we all took to our heels. I went to support Michel, but he pushed me off and said he could manage to get away safely.

There is nothing more to say about it all. Friends, whose names I do not intend to reveal, helped me to leave Rome and get here to Milan, my birthplace. I have friends here as well; they obtained work for me as a military architect. Does it seem strange that I should work for the Spaniards when you have heard what we thought of them in Rome? As I said, I no longer know anything about politics. Besides, an exile cannot afford to be choosy! I am efficient, I was with the army in Flanders many years ago. I know the handiwork of war. I have seen men die far more miserably than that fool Ranuccio: soldiers with the top of their head sliced off, with broken bones, hanging guts their comrades pushed back in place to spare the dying man the sight of them. Yes, and when the enemy fires cannon-balls chained together so they whizz through the air and the chain cuts everything in two, be it man or horse!

Well. I reconnoitre, make precise sketches of enemy fortifications and important towns. I can build bridges and earthworks, explode mines, dig trenches beneath enemy positions. If need be I can cope with gunnery and calculate ballistics. I act as a spy, am an explosives expert, an engineer and I am paid in Spanish gold. Can that be held against me? Surely the Spaniards are His Borghesian Holiness's best friends?

But I miss the city. And most of all I miss my friend the

painter, my countryman, my carousing companion Michel, Michel Angelo, the crazy Merisi from Caravaggio. We belong together, he and I, we are like brothers or at least cousins: our fathers were friends in their youth here in Lombardy. He managed to get to Naples, I heard tell; he too had to take refuge in Spanish country. And it is rumoured that he has been in Malta, with the Knights of St John. Well, that would suit him nicely! There are even some who say he has been admitted to the order, that he has become a knight, that if necessary he would fight for our holy Christian cause against the infidels. You know it is said that the Grand Master of La Valette in his time used the heads of Turkish prisoners to shoot back at the besieging force. That would have been something for Michel to paint! Yes, he really should have, ha ha ha . . .

Oh, dear! His Holiness sets store by good painters, I have heard tell. Beg him to pardon Michel, then he can enlarge his collection with the most splendid pictures. Ask him to forget politics, say he must turn a blind eye to Michel's conduct. Is a painter not more worthy for ever than the life of a soldier and brawler? And if he could really consider pardoning Michel, beg him in the friendliest way to include me in the bargain. All this is the fault of politics, but that kind of human pigheadedness doesn't interest me any longer, I say! White or black, French or Spanish, all the same to me. I am a Lombard by birth but a Roman by custom. I want to go back to Rome. I have done nothing wrong. I was merely unlucky enough to be present at that ridiculous scuffle on the playing field . . .

The Account of
Pater Giovan Battista Merisi

I HAVE BEEN asked to formulate an opinion regarding my brother, the murderer. I must emphasize that it is with the greatest reluctance, and only because I have been charged to undertake it, that I write these lines.

We come of a good Lombardian family. As far as I can remember our early childhood was generally happy until the year when my brother reached six years old and I myself five. Then we were struck down by the greatest of misfortunes: the plague took not only our father but also his parents.

It is bad for a boy to grow up without his father. I myself have felt this loss all my life, like an enigma to which I never found an answer, a cryptic text without any exegesis. What would my father have said now? What would he have done? Advised me to do?

But it must have been even worse for my brother Michel. A father whose hand was both gentle and strict might perhaps have led him into fitter paths from his childhood onwards. Indeed, I truly believe that. Our father was a respected man who worked for no less than the Colonna family, a man who could command respect. Mother – peace be with her blessed memory – reduced to poverty in widowhood, was unable to handle our upbringing, in particular where Michel was concerned. He had an obstinate and self-willed nature, which I as the youngest came to feel all too harshly. The painter's hands may hold his brush gently, but I can bear witness to their hardness as well.

So my brother was sent away to serve an apprenticeship with Master Simone of Bergamo, an honest and Christian painter, well regarded both for his altar-pieces and for his way of life. When Michel paid one of his rare visits home to us we got the impression that the two of them did not get on too well. The trouble was that the small boy could not refrain from criticizing his master's work, with the result that the artist had to take the birch to his disciple numerous times.

Well, then. Thus each of us grew up in his own way, until we finally parted. I have not seen my brother Michel Angelo for more than some few seconds in almost eighteen years, since the time when he, I and our sister Catarina shared out the scanty possessions that were our maternal inheritance. At that time he had just turned nineteen and been released from prison in Milan, where he had been incarcerated for several months during Mother's illness and death.

The prison sentence was the result of something that had taken place at one of the houses of ill repute in town. This is how it was related to me: a well-known citizen was carried out of the place unconscious, and a screaming whore lay inside with a knife wound that had cut her right eyeball in two and split her whole cheek down to the jaw. The man died at his home a few days later. But the whore recovered, even though her face was so disfigured that she must have had scant hope of resuming her shameful calling. (After all, perhaps there was some hidden mercy in that terrible event.)

The whore accused my brother and two other men of being responsible for the attack on the man and said that her own injuries were inflicted when she tried to stop the fight. My brother was immediately arrested but denied all knowledge of the case, and thus could not denounce his accomplices. As far as I am aware no form of torture was applied, perhaps on account of my brother's youth, more probably because evidence from a whore was not regarded as sufficiently reliable.

Anyhow, Michel Angelo was released after a few months, although the case was never really concluded. He at once demanded his share of the inheritance, as he wanted to leave our home town and go to Rome. By then I had already decided to devote my life to the Church.

As I said, I write this on the injunction of my superiors and not to excuse my brother. All the same it must be said that the months he spent in prison as a very young man changed and affected him severely. He was a heedless, far too boisterous youth when he got himself involved in this affair, fond of wine and with unsuitable friends, a defiant and boastful lad who out of all things in the world took only painting seriously. He came out a sombre grown man with a dark, hard laugh I had never heard from him before. I do not know what changed him so:

hopelessness, the company of hard-boiled criminals, the certainty that he was innocent – if that was so – but was not believed. The worst thing was that he had decided to give up his training as a painter.

Well, in Rome he took up painting again – he did not really have any choice, it was the only thing he could do. Naturally, rumours of his life reached me: whores, street brawls, arrests, scandalous paintings. I myself tried to live a life of unalloyed purity all this time; it was as if I had to make up for my brother, be the white sheep in the flock of the shepherd of souls, all the whiter as his blackness increased.

In my modest calling I have tried to comfort the sorrowful, forgive the fallen, collect the means of filling the hungry and clothing the cold. People have said, perhaps rightly, that I show too much forbearance to sinners, that I do not crack the whip of chastisement hard enough. Perhaps that was because I felt real responsibility for the one sinner who ought to be closest to me. As priest and brother it was up to me to urge him to improve.

I did once try to talk to him. For rumour had it that in some way or other he was involved in the notorious case of the Cenci family but was not called to account because there was no evidence against him. Some even claimed that he had been far too close a friend of the executed Beatrice, the patricide!

Naturally, this troubled me deeply. My brother, who himself had grown up without a father – surely he could never in any way have collaborated in making yet another family fatherless? True, they were only rumours, but the mere fact that such tales could arise. I travelled to the city and found the Palazzo Madama where he lived with a not unknown cardinal, who, I have to admit with great regret, did not enjoy a completely blameless reputation. I announced myself at the gate but after a few minutes was informed that my brother did not wish to speak to me. I sent in another message and emphasized that I had travelled a long way with this one meeting in mind.

Then I did get to see him, for a few seconds, as I mentioned earlier. The servant had left me to wait in the hall. Now Michel came down a great splendid staircase accompanied by a handsome young boy, dressed only in strange white flowing garments.

What he said – or, rather, shouted – to me down the staircase I have absolutely no wish to reveal. It must be enough to indicate that he made an exceptionally coarse reference to the relationship between Jesus Christ himself and the saint whose name I bear.*

That was my brother. The Lord must forgive me, but since that day I have felt no fraternity with this person who has the same father and mother as myself. We had not seen each other for ten years, I had undertaken a long journey to meet him – and he did not want to see me but sent me away with a vulgar obscenity for the sake of a moment's amusement for a young man.

When I heard about his final misfortune I at once came to the conclusion that it was due to heresy. A man who put his own

---

* Giovan (Giovanni) Battista is the Italian form of John the Baptist. (Editor's note)

capricious whims before the bonds of blood and family had naturally no respect either for the revealed and transmitted Truth. That was the only natural conclusion. This Ranuccio Tomassoni may have been a scoundrel, but he was obviously a good Christian. That was why he drew his sword against my brother, the blasphemer Michel Angelo Merisi from Caravaggio, to defend the sacred Catholic Faith and his own honour. I try to live a pure and simple life; my brother is a murderer and heretic who dishonours the Church by putting his own observations and notions above the sacred norms of decorum and decency.

After that incident I made another journey to the city. I may have been driven by profane curiosity, but I had to see *the pictures*. A murderer had fled, but in spite of everything we bore the same family name, a name that might live on by virtue of these paintings of his.

They merely confirmed my opinion. They are said to be 'good pictures'. And it is true that he can paint – imagine if this man had used his rich talents to paint *good pictures* in the spiritual sense! But his working method, the all too mechanical imitation of nature, is reminiscent of other heretical ideas of the time. If it were not that a drunken brawler like my brother can hardly know what is up and down in the firmament, much less the difference between a planet and a fixed star, one might well imagine him as an adherent to Kepler's dangerous ideas.

Although perhaps I am underestimating him here. One of his best friends in Rome is said to have been a notorious old bookseller on the Piazza Navona, who has been charged two or three times for having sold forbidden books. Even if Michel had not read them it is natural to think they would have talked of these heretical writings.

But nowhere did his heresy show itself more clearly than in his choice of models.

These rumours met me on my arrival in Rome. In particular there was talk of the picture of *The Death of the Virgin* commissioned by the Carmelites of Sta Maria della Scala. Apparently it depicted Our Holy Mother not in a blessed state of transition from the earthly to the heavenly sphere but as an ordinary common corpse, already swollen – as if Maria's holy body could not be spared from the brutal processes of physical death.

This in itself would be enough to make a pious man raise his sword against Michel.

Obviously the Carmelites could not use the work. It was sold, via a foreign speculator, undoubtedly a Lutheran, to an Italian prince – alas, one of those powerful figures who put earthly goods above heavenly truth.

I tried to find out more about this but was told there was only one person who could help me – but this was a woman who had known my brother extremely well. The snatches I heard made me feel, despite all my objections, that it was absolutely necessary to seek her out – Signorina Phyllida Melandroni.

I did not look forward to it. All over the town stories abounded about this ageing whore, how she had used her wiles to turn the head of a young and impressionable man by the name of Guilio Strozzi, who was being groomed to become chief notary to the papal chair. She had been exiled from Rome on Vatican orders, on the initiative of the young man's father.

But she was pardoned and had come back. She opened the door herself.

Phyllida Melandroni was still a beautiful woman. God keep my soul, but it struck me that the chief notary designate had perhaps not been so completely witless. I introduced myself and explained my errand.

'Will you come with me to Sta Maria sopra Minerva, Pater?' she asked.

It will be understood that I was not all that delighted to have to stroll through the city in company with a well-known, even if no longer young, cocotte in broad daylight. But if the woman had something of importance to tell me, and it had to be related in God's house, it was my duty to go along with her.

We walked together into the church which in my modest opinion may be the most beautiful in all Rome. The high vaulting and luminous blue colour of the ceiling immediately lead the mind to the heavenly spheres. Indeed, the proud pointed arches reach up directly to the Lord; they are like arrows pointing out the right way.

Phyllida Melandroni lit a candle before the altar where the Blessed Catherine's coffin rests. Then we sat down and she began to speak.

'You must hear the story of Anna Bianchini, that is what you are searching for. We came here together from Siena, Annuccia and I. She was chubby, red-haired, beautiful. We were fourteen years old when we were sent out on the streets here. Can you imagine it . . . ?'

I tried to imagine two fourteen-year-old girls, like those I know from my home village. I imagined them together, with their shy smiles and sudden laughter, still with the quick, angular movements of children. And I went on to visualize large, coarse male figures approaching those bodies that the day before had been children's, uttering terse brutal commands, tearing at their simple clothing, lewdly exposing that which seemliness and natural modesty should cover, throwing themselves upon them in shameless lust, ramming themselves against their thin bodies, penetrating *inside* them with violence.

They would leave the young girls lying prone with closed eyes, in a way still innocent in the midst of the degradation, before pressing ten or fifteen baiocchi into the little girlish hands helplessly clenched.

The thought was almost unbearable.

'No,' I replied, 'I cannot imagine such things.'

'I have come through it, as you see,' said Phyllida. 'In a way. I have had good protectors, I have been able to adapt myself. Annuccia was not so lucky. She had a few fairly good years while she was young and beautiful. But she was too angry, too proud, too high-spirited. She did have protectors, not in the highest circles but reliable men in good service. But all the same she took them to task, spoke angrily to them, accused them of pandering so they ended up in the pillory. They took revenge. One of them had her condemned to be publicly whipped.'

Phyllida closed her eyes. The great church was empty. Once again I looked up at the blue ceiling. The candle, which I now understood she had lit for her childhood friend from the hills of Siena, burned quietly before the altar.

A public whipping was the usual punishment for whoring.

'How did she die?' I asked.

'It was so terrible. She was expecting a child. But she fell so ill, swollen all over, her teeth fell out. Then she suffered cramps and screamed continuously before fainting away. I fetched a doctor to her, one of the costly ones. He said it was eclampsia* and tried blood-letting, but it did not help. Annuccia was dead before nightfall.'

'You did what you could for her,' I said.

'No, no, I should have fetched a priest! She never received the sacraments. She died without . . . Think what is happening to her now!'

I have to say that hearing how a corrupt woman such as this could have a care for her friend's soul in spite of everything made a great impression on me.

'You have seen the painting?' said Phyllida, '*The Penitent Magdalen*?'

'No, unfortunately,' I had to admit.

'It should really be called "The Chastised Annuncia",' said Phyllida. 'Yes, your brother painted her after the punishment! After she had been whipped on the Campo de'Fiori in front of a

---

* Toxaemia in pregnancy. (Editor's note)

crowd of people who yelled at her and scorned her. And no doubt then she repented too, just as much as the Blessed Magdalene, I imagine. But what was she to do afterwards? No Jesus was there to look after her – only Michel, who had nothing in his head but his picture.'

'He was not the father of her child?' I asked.

'I cannot imagine that. But he sat with her at the end. That made her happy, Annuccia, while she was still aware of things. In fact it was her last joy.'

'It was good of Michel to do that,' I said, surprised and slightly comforted.

Phyllida Melandroni began to weep again.

'I think so too,' she sobbed. 'I have thanked him many times. But later I came to understand why. It was not out of kindness, I assure you!'

'Now listen,' I said. 'What but true Christian sympathy can make a man sit by a woman's deathbed, a woman who is carrying another's child into the bargain?'

'Well, what do you think? Michel wanted to make use of her dead body, that's what made him do it!'

'What are you saying?' I shouted, for her words alarmed me so much I forgot we were on holy ground.

Phyllida stopped crying, dried her face and looked me straight in the face.

'He did use her. Even at the point of death she was not a human being to him, merely a body precisely as she was after the whipping. Do you not understand? A body, an object! A model!

He took note precisely of how death made its mark on her – he had need to know that, for he was engaged in painting *The Death of the Virgin*.'

If this was not heresy . . . That was my clear understanding of the matter. Only a single fact argued against it, but that in itself was enough to throw me into the greatest doubt.

It concerned yet another altar-piece, *The Madonna and Child with St Anne,** a commission for the Palafrenieri Brothers' chapel in the Vatican. I have never seen the painting, but evidently it was not to the Palafrenieri taste and was removed after a few days, as was generally the rule with Michel's altar-pieces.

I spoke to Brother Arnoldo who had helped to take down the painting. At first he did not wish to talk about it, especially when I introduced myself as the painter's sibling. He said curtly that there were several reasons which made it impossible for the picture to remain. Some thought the Blessed Anna looked like an old witch. Other brothers pointed out with great disgust – may our Blessed Mother preserve me from such sin, I merely repeat what was told to me – that the child Jesus was painted with far too conspicuous and prominent nakedness.

Then I remembered that something similar had been said of other paintings of Michel's.

But there were theological objections as well. Brother Arnoldo explained that the altar-piece shows the Blessed Mother of God crushing the head of the serpent with her naked foot,

---

* This is a representation of Christ, the Virgin Mary and her mother Anne. (Editor's note)

with some slight help from the child, while the Blessed Anna merely looks on. Several of the brothers had believed that this indicated a dangerous adaptation of de Molina's ideas on human freedom. It went without saying that the theological and thereby iconographically correct situation was that the Blessed Anna also had to take part if sin was to be overcome, as a representative of divine grace, for otherwise human beings would be capable of saving themselves! That, Arnoldo considered, was a natural consequence of Anna's being made pregnant by the Holy Spirit.

Truth to tell, I did not fully understand this interpretation of the picture, and as a modest and unlearned village priest I have no clear understanding of de Molina's theology either, so I merely answered respectfully that the Immaculate Conception of Jesus was as clear as day, but where the question of how the Virgin in her time conceived again was concerned I would bow to every plausible authoritative interpretation, as this question could hardly be said to involve the innermost core of the Faith.

Brother Arnoldo did not seem too pleased with my answer, so I hastened to add that that also agreed with the opinion I held of my brother's life and work – heretical ideas everywhere. This made the brother nod earnestly, and we sat in silence together for a while.

But before I left I had to ask him to describe the Maria of the picture. The good brother gave me a detailed description of a stately, black-haired young woman with a slightly triangular face and well-marked almost straight eyebrows, who had generous breasts and slim, high-arched feet. I could not help thinking that all the same the picture had made a certain impression on the good Arnoldo in the course of the brief time it had hung in the chapel, but I also felt some relief at hearing that *this* Virgin could be neither Phyllida nor her red-haired friend Annuccia.

Then it was that Arnoldo said something that made my entire conviction waver.

'Luckily the brotherhood did not lose anything over the affair. We paid that Caravaggio seventy-five scudi, but we managed to sell the picture for a hundred!'

'That was not bad,' I replied and thought what it must be like to *own* a hundred scudi. I thought of the poorest people in my village, who had never owned a larger sum than four or five baiocchi, indeed, had hardly *seen* a single scudo in their whole lives.

'We feared the worst,' Arnoldo went on. 'For this was just after that brutal scene on the Campo Marzio. The painter had fled, and we thought that perhaps no one would dare to buy such a dubious picture, painted by – now, you must forgive me, Pater Merisi – a runaway murderer!'

'There is no need for forgiveness,' I replied. 'Unfortunately. But who bought the picture? A foreign ambassador, a Lutheran, perhaps?'

'The Lutherans have no money,' sniffed Arnoldo. 'No, the painting did not go *so* far away from St Peter's Church. It is now part of the Borghese fortune.'

We sat talking on a bench in the shade, Brother Arnoldo and I. But at the sound of that name I could no longer remain seated.

I rose and shouted: 'Which Borghese? Surely His Holiness himself has not seen fit to buy a heretical work!'

'Not exactly,' replied Arnoldo. 'But certainly his favourite nephew, not that that is any great improvement.'

'The cardinal?'

'Cardinal Scipione Caffarelli Borghese himself came and insisted on having the picture. Truth to tell, we would probably have let it go for seventy-five if he had pressed us.'

After this I left Rome at once and went home. If my clear and compelling conviction of the heretical character of my brother's work and actions does not agree with the opinion of the very highest men in the Holy Church, those men I ought to love, esteem and obey as the Lord himself, there is nothing I can do about it other than remain modestly in the background as is seemly, saying as little as possible, preferably keeping silent.

Thus I end my account, once more emphasizing that it was written with no initiative whatsoever on my part.

The Account of
Phyllida Melandroni

To whom it may concern:

I, Phyllida Melandroni, have nothing whatsoever to do with either the painter, Michel Angelo from Caravaggio, said to have left this city a long time ago, or with Ranuccio Tomassoni from Terni, said to have been killed by the painter before he disappeared. I do not know what kind of dispute or enmity had arisen between these two gentlemen, whom I knew only slightly many years ago.

For that matter, I may be permitted to say that I find it extremely strange that I, who was exiled from Rome and threatened with imprisonment and excommunication, not to speak of public whipping, have been requested to give evidence in a case such as this. Neither the authorities of the Church nor the city have previously had the slightest faith in me. Now all I wish for is to live in peace, go to confession and repent of the sins I have committed.

Moreover, both Michel Angelo and Ranuccio are two unpredictable and choleric men who do not need any particular reason to let fly at each other. Both are reckless and immoderate with drink, both have friends who egg them on rather than calm them down. But I am sure the police archives speak more eloquently about this than I can, so there is no reason for me to say more.

Then, both of them are men who make use of women, each in his own way. At any rate, Tomassoni previously offered his 'protection' to one or two of those miserable creatures among us who have to earn their living by the means that nature has put at a woman's disposal. Well, a lot of protection that was! 'Pimp' would be a more suitable word for a man who sees to it, it is true, that a woman is not beaten completely to death but who, on the other hand, makes gross use both of her purse and her body.

Merisi the painter is still worse. His very bearing is such that women desire to please him. He does not swagger up and slap you on the thigh like other men; he sits down beside you and gazes into your face. He does not address you coarsely or try to kiss you by force; he just says something about your eyes or hair. Other foolish fellows take the greatest pleasure in getting hold of a woman's breasts; the painter strokes your neck lightly or draws a finger carefully down over your cheek, with an almost shy hand, as he rises to take his leave. He can certainly swear, yell and hit out – and the cause need not be more than his losing a game of pallacorda – but he fights with other men, never with women. Well – anyhow, *almost* never.

His appearance is not better or healthier than many other men, but his figure is taut and at the same time supple. He speaks *to* you as if you were the only one in the world who interested him just at that moment. And his features are serious, with a melancholy as if he is bravely enduring a secret sorrow. Women notice such things.

In short, the painter is a man who attracts women. And then comes the day when he says: 'Now you must let me paint you.'

No one who has not been a model can understand this, and I do not intend to enlarge on it, because it is of no interest in this case. But to see your own figure appear, to know you have been captured for ever in this moment and will be there before people's eyes for ever, whether on the wall of a cardinal or above the altar in a church, that is a feeling unlike any other.

But this, of course, is trickery. *Nothing* is eternal, apart perhaps from judgement and mercy. Inevitably, another time will come, a time when you will not spend hours in the painter's warm room with the faint scents of his colours and oils, with the light falling from a skylight he has had built in high above, with the long hours when his gaze rests on you, sees you as no one has ever been seen before, hours when you are transformed into something different, into a picture, into someone who finds herself on the other side of sin and wickedness and death.

Another will take your place. This is the way of the world; it is inconstant, changing, vain. The one thing we can be sure of is that nothing lasts. We know this well enough, but we will never comprehend it – I believe we would hardly manage to go on living if we really looked this knowledge in the face. Another will take your place, and you are out in the darkness where there is no warmth, scents or colours. Yes, you are outside in the dark, and the suffering makes you experience everything more sharply than ever: you feel, smell and see what it is like in that room, you know exactly what is going on there – and you know *you* are not the one in there, but another.

Cast off, alone, empty, annihilated. For all I know this is merely the earthly foretaste of eternal damnation, where punishment is not so much glowing tongs and lakes of burning fire but the pain of being one of the condemned, one of those the Lord has rejected.

But this is not relevant to the case. It is unimportant to me whether the painter Merisi is pardoned or not. The only thing I would ask is to be spared any more such interrogations as this. This is actually the second one I have suffered – some time ago a shabby country priest who claimed to be the painter's brother came and asked me a whole lot of questions, among them one about a deceased woman friend of mine. I received him politely and tried sincerely to explain to him the circumstances of our coming here from Siena. But when I mentioned, with deep sorrow, how as mere children we had been sent out to a life of sin, I saw a smile full of lust spread over the priest's face. That ageing pater was obviously drawn to the idea of having his filthy way with innocent young girls. At least his brother was not as corrupt as that. All I ask is to be left in peace. For the time I have left.

The Account of
Maddalena Antognetti

'I AM LENA from the Piazza Navona, Michel Angelo's woman.'

'That is what I said in court, as if the judge was a father confessor ordering me to come out with the secrets of my heart, as if he could not be satisfied with the outside, the bruised face, the marks around the eyes that will probably never go away.

I am Lena who lives in the Via dei Greci and was once Gasparc Albertini's woman.

I am Lena who lives in the house of my sister Amabilia; Cesare Barattieri's woman, Cardinal Allesandro's woman, Monsignor Melchiorre Crescenzi's woman, Guilio Massini's woman, Ranuccio Tomassoni's woman . . .

I am Maddelena Antognetti, twenty-eight years old and soon to die. Father Andrea has been here. He would not give me divine unction and absolution until Mother and Amabilia offered to pay him threefold. I find this reasonable, as reasonable as the fact that life is running out of me through the very orifice where sin found entrance. The misdeeds carry the punishment within them. If only there had not been so much blood. The work of mopping it up makes my sister tired and irritable, I hear it in her voice although she tries to hide it.

Yet my greatest sin is not that I opened my body to far too many men, that I bore a child without knowing who the father was, not even that I deceived that idiot Gaspare, who was genuinely fond of me in his foolish way, provided I complied with his preposterous notions. My greatest sin – and this is what must be related here in my final hours – is that I was the one who brought misfortune upon Michel Angelo.

Oh yes, I know. His own unreasonable mind, the excess of yellow bile that ran in his veins, he himself contributed to what happened. But without me things would not have gone disastrously wrong so fast, and perhaps the artist would still be living here in Rome instead of roaming about foreign lands, persecuted and miserable.

God will look mercifully upon me for my many men; He knows I have never known any other trade than that of the courtesan, the hetaera or the whore. My mother had a house on the Corso, thanks to money from my father. My father was a cardinal whose name I have sworn never to reveal, a servant of God addicted to drink who used far too much of his small fortune on my mother. I do not think the Lord himself can have hit upon anything as foolish as celibacy. Surely he must know that it drives the wifeless men of the Church crazy, so they show less concern for Him but use their strength and mind and not least their money to get hold of a pair of willing thighs they can empty themselves between, those who are not lucky enough to be content with the backsides of choirboys.

I grew up in the house on the Corso. As a little girl I saw how Mother and Amabilia received men – indeed they made me join in their shameful games from the age of five or six, when I was quite unaware they were shameful. My mother, whom I respected and honoured, my beloved big sister – when these my nearest and dearest took me with them to the merry gentlemen, laughingly set me on strangers' laps and praised me for my precocious antics, how could I think that wrong? When I sat across the fat thighs of the men, snuggled up to their swollen stomachs and rocked playfully up and down, I was not scolded or beaten but rewarded with cheers and maybe a coin.

To be sure, I am guilty, but the Lord will look mercifully on me for that. But that my vanity and profligate actions misled an artist into drawing his sword on the Campo Marzio, for that there may well be no pardon.

I must be brief. My strength is almost gone, I cannot see clearly. But the pains are the same. I will ask my sister to bring me a sip of wine; it soothes and strengthens. The story must be told just as it is.

Michel needed me for two reasons. Because I was beautiful – I state it plainly, as I lie here now, pale, withered, shrunken and sullied – and because I had a son.

I could have refused – I *ought* to have refused. He wanted to use me as a model for the Mother of God and my poor Paolo would represent the Child! The Blessed Maria and the lost Lena; all we probably had in common was that neither of us really knew who might be the father of our sons.

But I didn't refuse. I valued the few baiocchi I would be able to earn in this easy way more than the fear of the sin I would burden myself with by lending my outward form to a picture of her. I sold my body, in this as in other ways.

Naturally I lied to Gaspare. That was a sin as well, one should not lie even to a dull-witted fool like him. After all, he had taken me into his house as his regular woman, me, the whore from the Corso! There I could give the impression of a virtuous matron, have a little money for food and clothes, go to market and nod to the others, although I was well aware that they looked down on me. But I had a man, a notary, no less, who earned his living in the courts, certainly not a bark-stained tanner or stinking fishmonger. I should not have reproached him for not taking me to the altar – he was, after all, not *that* stupid.

A man, my man; a man who demanded no more than that I looked after his clothes, cooked the meals and pretended to enjoy his weird games. Dear God, surely I could dress him up in a child's clothes, tie him to the bed and whip him, pretend to be his mother and wash him all over, since it gave him so much pleasure!

Instead I went off to the painter, and I told myself it was for the sake of the money. But that is a lie too. For just a few baiocchi Michel Angelo took my form, and Paolo's, when I took him with me, and implanted us on the canvas for the staircase of Sta Casa, the holy house of Loreto. Well, it was business: I gave, he took – but I would gladly have done it for nothing. For when I saw how the work of capturing my beautiful features in oil aroused him, I made him free of my body in the other way too, the one I knew only too well.

And that was without any payment. Some have said that Merisi, the painter from Caravaggio, is not one who takes pleasure in women. If anyone can witness to his advantage on this point it has to be me. For I can truly say that his stamina was as impressive as in any other man I have known. He could paint me without pause. I stood there before him as Maria the Immaculate for two hours or more. Then he came to me. He took off my lovely, red-brown silk blouse and began to kiss me passionately all over the upper part of my body, constantly repeating my name.

Now I am lying, I who have but a few hours or days before I shall meet with that judge who will allot me a place in eternity. When you have spent a whole life in the lie known as purchased love, it is pretty hard to die in the truth. But I must try: it was not *my* name he uttered while he kissed me, undressed me, caressed me – for it was not the model he embraced but the subject.

In the first picture he finished, the one that hangs now in Sant'Agostino, the two weary pilgrims kneel piously before Maria and the Child. The light falls so gently, particularly on the face of the old woman, that you can *see* how the blessing of the Mother of God pours down upon her.

Many were offended by the picture. The two wayfarers are too poor, too unworthy, the man has dirty feet turned directly towards the observer. But no one had anything to say about the figure of Maria other than that she is so beautiful she must reflect divine grace. Ha! The figure standing there is mine, a few moments before the artist lays down his brush and comes towards me.

Yes, it was I who gave him the capacity to fill this Maria with beauty; it was my sensuality that set fire to his brush. He was driven by an insatiable need for my body. He painted like one in fever or delirium, for as long as he could go on. Then he knelt down before me, spread my legs and called me *Maria*. 'Make room for The Holy Ghost!' he shouted and licked a sign of the cross on my naked body from the throat to the fork, from the left to the right breast.

The picture was finished. The pious Augustinians did not look at the dirty feet but paid Michel and hung it up in their church. I myself did not dare look at it there, afraid that someone might suddenly cry out that the dark, upright Maria with her shy glance and beautiful, almost straight eyebrows far too much resembled the whore kneeling below at prayer; even more afraid that suddenly lust would show itself in *her* face, infected by my own unworthiness.

But it was only then that the fuss began. Naturally Gaspare came to hear about the picture, and rushed off to see it. That night he beat me for the first time, and again later on when I refused to play with him – it was just before I developed a certain respect for the pale notary. He beat me until I had to confess I had posed as the model and promise to stay away from the painter from Caravaggio for ever afterwards.

How could I do that? How could I stay away from that man

with fire in his eyes and his limbs, he who had *seen* me, captured Lena the whore with his gaze and his brush and turned her into the queen of heaven for a moment? What if Michel Angelo did have other women and not only women. People said that his young lad of a servant also served his master with his childish slender body, but what could I say against that? When he called, I came.

I put on men's clothes and slipped out after Ave Maria, to the places where the painter waited. He painted me again, as the Virgin in his *Madonna and Child with St Anne*, in the same manner as before.

No, worse than before. I am going to die, I must tell the truth. One day he made old 'Anna' with her wrinkles and hanging breasts undress and join in. He had both of us. And I went along with it.

One evening on the Corso a *sbirro* recognized and arrested me. I said I was Gaspare's woman, on my respectable way home, and that I had promised the notary to keep away from all other men, especially Michel.

Gaspare beat me and then restored me to favour. But I didn't manage to stay away from Michel – and to tell the truth he didn't make it easy for me. He waylaid me in the street, arranged rendezvous. Gaspare's friends told him everything. They said I gave him such large and visible horns that he would have to throw me out. But he was too stupid to do that. He made Mother and Amabilia promise that *they* would keep me away from the painter. Yes, they listened to him and not to me! They thought

I was mad to fornicate for nothing with a painter when I could get food and clothes by merely going along with the notary's simple requirements. He may perhaps have paid them something to guard me; he even believed that would work. As if *they* could control me.

In the end he sent me home to them on the Corso, made a prison for me. What an idea! Of course Michel came, scolded Mother, then let fly at the neighbour, Laura the fruiterer, who came to help Mother throw him out. The next night when he came back Mother did not open the door at all – then he broke his way into Laura's house, drunk and furious.

I am going to die. And the Lord must forgive me, but I have never been so proud of myself as when I was locked into a room without windows but could still hear the uproar outside. It was Michel Angelo, an artist whose name was on everyone's lips all around town, whose paintings were purchased by men of high standing – and he was bellowing and hitting out, kicking and cursing down there, because he was not allowed to come to *me,* because he was not permitted to embrace *my* slim body with his eyes and his arms.

Later, everything went wrong. Gaspare came and gave me a beating, my nose was broken. Of course Laura went to the authorities, and the police searched for Michel. Some of his friends intervened. God knows who they had to bribe, not rich people; there were one or two painters, a tailor and the book-seller on the Piazza Navona. They promised to keep Michel away from the Corso and the fruiterer. Mother and Amabilia had to move over here to the Via dei Greci, while I was allowed to live with the bookseller, so Michel knew where he could find me.

The bookseller is an elderly man with a dignified grey beard. All the same, he was no different from other men. He did not allow my broken nose to stop him. He demanded his rent from me on the days when Michel could not come, after first pouring me a drink that was neither wine nor grappa but tasted strong and sickly at the same time. He kept it locked up and took a glass or two only when some of his friends came round. The drink made me dizzy and slightly numbed, so that I could almost forget Michel when the bookseller's old, hairy body slumped over mine. I did not dare say anything about this to the painter. Perhaps he knew about it – the two of them were friends, after all – or perhaps he did not. And no one could foresee what he would do next.

Anyway, the drink dulled the pain in my nose for a while. In the end I began to *ask* the bookseller for some, even though I had to take him as well.

I tried to report Gaspare because he had disfigured me and because he had taken a married woman as his lover in my place, the old whoremonger. But naturally the court listened to him, a notary.

One evening in October Michel came staggering in with a big wound on his head. I washed away the blood and saw his skull shining white in the wound. Michel fainted away in my arms, but the bookseller bandaged him and got some of that drink into him, which livened Michel up. Gaspare's friends had lain in ambush for him, possibly with the Tomassoni brothers, whom I had also known at one time. But when the police arrived Michel would not say who had attacked him, even though the wound might easily have cost him his life. I think he was ashamed because he had been taken by surprise and had not defended himself better.

Thus the winter passed. My nose did not heal; Michel did not come so often.

Then came the day when Ranuccio Tomassoni challenged him to a duel on the Campo Marzio. And that was my fault. Gaspare must have been behind it all in some way or other. And Michel used me to stir up that boor Ranuccio, who long ago had been my friend and protector. I heard later what he had yelled.

'I've never lost a game of ball to a pimp and cocksucker. Do you remember the beautiful Lena? If you'd been anything of a man you would have kept her for yourself instead of leaving her to that nitwit of a notary I had to rescue her from.'

And when Ranuccio told him to take that back or fight, Michel replied, and the words are so typical of him I can *hear* his voice: 'There's nothing to win for a man of honour fighting someone like you. You had better look out for yourself, Ranuccio! You've already lost your balls, why do you want your head off as well?'

That sort of thing could only end in a duel, two men against each other for life or death. And of course Michel won, even though Ranuccio was a boor and a warrior.

Soon I shall stand before a greater and, I hope, more just judge than the one I met in the Corte Savela when I tried to report Gaspare. But I shall give the same answer as then, when asked who I am.

'I am Lena from the Piazza Navona, Michel Angelo's woman.'

The Account of
Prospero Orsi, Painter

IT MUST BE understood that I am a Roman.

When I go out of the door of my family's old house on the Piazza S. Salvatore in Campo, I constantly meet people from Lombardy, Tuscany, Mantua or Naples. They come to Rome for many reasons, but above all because there is no other city like it in all the world.

They say there are many more inhabitants of Naples. There is far more wealth in Genoa and Venice; Florence and Siena resemble two exquisitely made gems adorning the loveliest landscape in the world.

That may well be. But, all the same, this is the place people come to. When I walk out of the house I can slip down through the alleyways to the Ponte Sisto, walk out on the bridge, lean my arms on the railings and look up along the Tiber. There is a moment, early in the morning if the weather is clear, when the grey water suddenly catches all the light of the sky and becomes a shining blue ribbon. The fishermen in their small boats are rocked by this light. I raise my eyes and see the top of Sant'Angelo in the distance, the sacred castle of the Angel defending our city for ever.

Urbi et orbi.* The light that streams out from this city shines all over the world. This was the centre of the world in the time of the Caesars that we can still see from the magnificent buildings they erected and from Marcus Aurelius where he holds sway high on horseback on the Capitol. Here the Holy Father raises his sceptre, and all the world trembles.

Here all must come who wish to distinguish themselves, for good or ill. That Titan Michelangelo Buonarotti had to leave the vainglorious provincial town of Florence and come to Rome. Bramante the architect was a great man in Milan, yet he travelled here. Even most of the popes themselves come from other places.

But here they are bound to come to attain to the throne.

The holiest men are to be found here. Among them the good Philip Neri, also from Florence, a man who was a saint even in his earthly life; we called him the Apostle of Rome. He would go out into the catacombs to pray the whole night long and then go to his church to comfort the poor all day. He could wring money out of the meanest cardinals, heal the most hopelessly sick, joke merrily with his brothers in the Faith and then be transported for hours in an ecstasy that tore and jerked at his poor body.

But the secret of Rome is the sparkling light *and* the ominous shade. The old people said that it was a short way from the Capitol of power to the humiliating death at the Tarpeian cliffs – and

---

* For the city and the world. (Editor's note)

the man who comes to Rome will discover that this is true of the city itself. Here is the shortest possible way from Philip Neri's oratory to the houses where the leading whores sit shamelessly outside graciously acknowledging nods and greetings from the citizens; indeed, even to reach the top rank in this godless profession it is necessary to come to Rome!

Without Rome the painter Michel Angelo Merisi would not have attained such perfection as he did in his work; but neither would he have committed such outrages.

I am a Roman myself. I see this more clearly than others. And you should know that no one living in Rome now knows the painter as well as I do.

When I first met him he was a lad in his early twenties, shabby and so poor that he could not afford colours, oils or brushes. He had worked in the studio of a wretched dauber by the name of Pandolpho, who could not recognize natural talent even when it was in front of his nose. Pandolpho was supposed to instruct the lad – and set him to copy his own feeble efforts! An even more disgraceful thing was that this dabbler was so tight-fisted that he fed his workers solely on lettuce – for starter, main course and dessert, Michel always said later, and he amused himself by annoying Pandolpho if they met in the street. Then he ran after his former master shouting: 'Monsignor Lettuce! Monsignor Lettuce! Have you had your supper yet?'

Michel left the fool and tried to manage without a master. He painted a few small pictures which were sold in bookshops, but then he caught malaria and ended up in the Spedal della Consolazione. I happened to see some of his pictures and immediately realized that here was something new.

What did this new thing consist of? It has been said that he 'paints from nature'. That is true enough, but it is not actually the secret. Merisi did not merely paint from nature; his eyes were sharper than others'. Or more childlike, if you will. He *saw* the subject itself as it was, with fresh eyes, as if it was the *first time* anyone had seen such a motif. He did not see the subject as it ought to be – or, as many do, through a thin glass membrane of habit.

He saw it anew, where other painters merely see how things have been painted before.

This is a more difficult art than anyone who has not tried for themselves can know.

When he was discharged from hospital he had nothing. In short, I took care of him. I gave him some painting equipment and took him on at my studio, arranged for a wealthy man to provide accommodation – and, not least, I showed his pictures to everyone who would look at them and to a good few who had never expressed a wish to.

He irritated many of our colleagues from the very start. Partly because he was arrogant, true enough. But also because he made them jealous. And jealous painters say so much. Some maintain that he paints dark or draped backgrounds because he cannot really achieve perspective. But don't they see that all his best works are *scenes*; that it is a structure he is creating, not to reproduce a reality but to intensify it?

Ah, well. Michel was a somewhat immature artist when I met him, but he quickly made progress. And he was not satisfied with doing the same things as others. He had new ideas. He used a mirror and painted self-portraits. He almost used the methods of a scientist as he eagerly studied vases half full of water – he wanted to understand reflections, refractions and the strange effects of light that follow these, in order to make his pictures as true to nature as possible. In his *nature morte* he showed this uncanny ability to render surfaces, as if he painted with the sense of touch instead of with the aid of sight, as we others have to do. He began to include glass bowls and vases in these pictures at this time. I supported him by selling several of them.

One day I gave him a large canvas with the beginnings of a madonna I was dissatisfied with. A sizeable canvas was still quite a treasure to him. He painted over my sketch and himself created a remarkable picture of a beautiful gypsy woman engaged in reading the hand of a delighted young nobleman. He had found his models at the nearest inn, of course. The painting turned out most successfully, and I hung it in my studio. It was purchased by a certain Alessandro, who, however, refused to give more than eight scudi for it. I protested, but Michel himself was only too glad to get a few coins in his hands.

Nevertheless the gypsy painting was to transform his life completely. At that time, eminent ecclesiastics never visited artists' studios themselves; instead, they sent their servants to inspect, or used intermediaries. So you will understand how astonished I was some days later when a cardinal appeared larger than life for the first time in my humble rooms, with only a pair of attendants accompanying him. Well, he had not had to stroll so far in his elegant silken garments, for he was in fact the lord of the Palazzo Madama, Franscesco Maria Bourbon del Monte.

I have to admit that I was a little disappointed when I realized that it was not the fame of *my* pictures that had lured the cardinal to visit. He had seen Michel's gypsy picture hanging at Alessandro's house and bought it on the spot. Now he wanted to see more.

That was how life changed for my young friend. From then on del Monte not only bought most of what he painted; the cardinal also commissioned the most varied subjects and paid well for the pictures. But it was not merely money, it was a closed world Michel was now given a glimpse of, the world of palaces, of ambassadors, the Curia. Del Monte gave Michel gifts so that in spite of his humble birth and position he could take his place here: clothes, boots – and a sword. Through the cardinal Michel met several of the leading men in Rome, although this did not prevent him from enjoying the company of whores and petty thieves at the inns.

But he changed character. You might think that contact with a high prelate would make him quieter and more serious. For through del Monte he was naturally assigned to paint pictures of saints and Bible figures. As far as I know, Michel had never painted a single such subject before *The Penitent Magdalen*. I don't think he had even considered it. But after Magdalene he painted religious themes almost exclusively. Moreover, he often had discussions with the Oratorians, Philip Neri's pious successors, who preach poverty and peace. I think he listened to their opinions, for once I heard him say that the people in his pictures ought to be simple, poor folk, whatever cardinals and others thought of such, for as we know, it is written: 'Blessed are the poor; for of such is the Kingdom of Heaven.'

In spite of this pious influence on his mind, at the same time he grew more hot-tempered, impetuous and touchy than before. The police began to take note of him – unfortunately not without reason.

I have tried to understand this change in him, which happened after he had moved into the cardinal's house. I think it was because Michel Angelo Merisi is not like other painters.

As I mentioned, he sees and feels his subjects in a new way, as if they have never been painted before. This is why he comes out with these arrogant comments on why he has not learned from others. In one sense this is true. In a way he paints like a child: he *is* in the subject.

As long as the subjects were worldly sketches and *nature morte*, all went well. But the great subjects were too much for him, no matter how much piety he originally possessed at the start of his work.

Crucifixion and death. Such things cause the humours to boil over in a painter who himself suffers when he paints suffering, who is repelled to the point of sickness by the scenes of death that arise under his hand. When he has been painting for several days or weeks, his suffering soul is so agonized by this that he has to escape from it all. He rages off like a bolting horse on the Corso; in its blind rush it runs down everything that gets in its way.

There are all too many instances of how Merisi's tortured mind led him into misfortune. Let me describe just one of them here. We are at an inn at the end of the Via Condotti. Then one of us gets the ill-fated idea that we want to eat artichokes – we have seen fresh ones in the market this very day. The landlord nods and goes to carry out the order, we drink some more and wait, and a quarter of an hour later a young apprentice comes in with a dish of glistening green artichokes, whose leaves curve mouthwateringly with the promise of pale, fleshy morsels at the end of each – and not least a meltingly soft core we can slowly work our way down to.

But meanwhile something has happened to Michel's liver, or a devil has flown into his restless soul. It *is* hard to cook artichokes perfectly. Perhaps the first one he tries is slightly too hard, perhaps it has the kind of rather bitter tang artichokes can sometimes have.

Whatever it is, he gives a yell and hurls the piping hot vegetable into the face of the boy, who has not yet managed to get back to the kitchen.

The lad gets badly burned, and for a while he loses the sight of one eye.

Mayhem erupts and fighting: the host defends his young employee, he defends his artichokes, he sends someone out to find a *sbirro*. Unfortunately a policeman happens to be standing only a few steps from the inn. Michel is arrested. Again there is talk of this ill-fated long sword he just *has* to carry and which in the end is to be his great misfortune. Michel is kept in captivity overnight; we others get off, but I have to go to del Monte straight away and call him from his bed. The cardinal is not too pleased – the litany he rattles off is not to be found in any missal.

Nevertheless he intervenes yet again. Michel gets out, with a black eye – he had a fight with a fellow prisoner and is angry with me because I did not get myself arrested with him.

Oh, there is more of this. The police reports must be full of abuse, trouble-making, affrays, use of weapons. The remarkable thing is probably not that Michel Angelo of Caravaggio killed a man on the Campo Marzio but that he himself had not been killed in a fight, executed on the Ponte Sant'Angelo or at least sent to the galleys.

But other painters have had this kind of imbalance in the humours without becoming murderers. Moreover, Michel Angelo was a provincial lad who had become a Roman.

Rome itself was to be his undoing. This unbridled fury, this tortured sensibility which made him liable to draw his sword at a trifling remark or an imagined insult – this can only be the uncertainty of the provincial youth. All the years when the whores hurled pert comments on his dialect before he learned to answer them back; when the landlords of inns served him the worst cuts of meat because, after all, he was a dim-witted peasant boy; when conceited painters like Pandolpho asked patronizingly where on earth he had somehow learned to draw.

I don't know what happened down there on the Campo Marzio. There is so much talk, most of it rumours, guesses and fictitious tales. Rome is like that, of course. A piece of news cannot run naked and clean through the streets – it grows and takes on the most extraordinary forms. As soon as it has travelled just a few districts away hardly anyone can recognize it behind the colours, filth and excrescences. But if I am asked about it, I believe those who say that Ranuccio Tomassoni made some remark about Merisi's background. Some claim he shouted that Merisi was a ham-fisted peasant's son, a mountain ape from Lombardy who would never learn to play decent *pallacorda*.

I know very well that the painter could kill for such a comment.

If he is to be pardoned, then it must be for Rome's sake.

This man will advance the reputation of our city. It is said that now he is painting wonderful pictures in Naples and already has a school of enthusiastic devotees and pupils down there in that overgrown, malaria-ridden marsh town. Is there any meaning in such a thing?

Let him come back. I do not say that for his own sake, but the city's. We need him, now more than ever.

Some have said I was his teacher. He needed no teacher, and anyway he would not have one. In any case, it would sound unnecessarily conceited of me – since Michel's reputation, even in his absence, far outshines my own here in Rome – to announce myself as this man's teacher. But let us say that I discussed the secrets of drawing with him and made him realize both its necessity and its limitations, and so helped him on his way. Michel Angelo is the man for colours, not for drawing. He renders the substance and density of things with the aid of nuances in the mixing of colours he defines contours by opposing colours rather than by drawing. There are some who consider drawing to be the soul of painting. Such rubbish has been taught out at St Luke's Academy: painting has a soul which the painter must capture in his sparse, almost spiritual lines before he can give it body with the aid of earthly and worldly colour.

It has been said that Michel is not a really great painter because he cannot draw well enough. It is true that there are better draughtsmen, including some here in Rome. These finical lacemakers may sit there scratching away at their soul-strokes, but what good does that do them when bodies and objects require surfaces? Michel does not *paint* glass, skin, clothes – he *creates* them. That is where his greatness lies. Certainly a painting may have a soul, but it *must* have a body.

The Account of
Peter Paul Rubens, Painter

THE ACCOUNT THAT follows has been written in an independent hand, in somewhat demotic Italian, with an arbitrary orthography which seems to have been influenced by a Teutonic language. Peter Paul Rubens left Rome on 28 October 1608, while the investigation must have taken place in 1610. The genuineness of the report cannot be ruled out on linguistic grounds, as it may have been written by Rubens himself and sent to Rome. (Editor's note)

I spent six happy years at the court of the Grand Duke of Mantua. His Excellency Vincenzo was gracious enough not merely to accept with pleasure the pictures that I myself painted, he also sent me out to see other artists' work, partly so that I should learn more, and partly to ensure that his own collections should be as good as possible.

Unfortunately, during my stay in Rome I only met the painter Merisi personally on one occasion, and at the time he was temporarily unable to work. Then, his technique was rather unoriginal. He still used a dark, even background instead of the more lively *imprimitura*, and his use of white lead to obtain the sharp light he aimed for was extremely immoderate. So I hardly think I had anything directly to learn from this artist, but I was a young man thirsting to make progress, and naturally I should have liked to see him at work.

Some time after our only meeting he was obliged to leave the city on account of the circumstances that have occasioned this document. I must admit that his fate greatly preoccupied me. I was not alone in this. At that time one could hardly take a step in the streets of Rome without hearing someone discussing what had actually taken place on the Campo Marzio.

We know God has singled out some individuals. Since our understanding is so immeasurably incomplete compared with His, we must reckon that in human eyes this predestination, this preordained selection, may well look as if the Lord is capricious, unpredictable in His whims. To be chosen, to be bound to a destiny, cannot be any easy fate, I imagine. But the chosen one can do nothing about that, other than tug at the rope of his destiny as strongly as he can. Again – seen from the human viewpoint – this may seem strange, the elected one's frantic dance to escape the will that still holds him fast. I believe this person's life would be incomprehensible if one did not see that all these grotesque, convulsive movements, these violent diatribes and compromising notions, are grouped around the unseen centre to which the rope is fastened: the destiny.

During my time in Rome I frequently strolled through the alleyways around the Piazza Navona. I often passed the place where the Blessed Agnes is said to have suffered martyrdom.

This led me to think of Merisi. Why did he never paint *that* scene, with his sense of the overcharged, the sensational: Agnes, devoted to God, captured, stripped naked in all her youthful virginity, dragged into the brothel on this piazza, where her hair grew so miraculously long to cover her shame!

The story is consoling and tells how the Lord protects his own. But it could also be rendered shocking enough in all its holiness, something of which Caravaggio obviously had so much understanding.

But he never painted Agnes's young body as it trembled behind a merciful curtain of hair. The fact is that he never painted nude women; only the naked Cupid, the young John in the desert, the boy Isaac on the altar where his father was about to sacrifice him. No one who has thoroughly studied his work can doubt that he takes great pleasure in these slim young boys with their soft skin and long, lithe limbs. A gentle warmth quivers through them which is lacking in the beautiful, cool female figures.

Ah, well. I often walked down to the Tiber by the Tor di Nona, the prison. Here, too, he had been imprisoned – it may have been precisely in this fearful place that he was sent after being sentenced for slander, that was discussed so much at the court of Mantua. And His Excellency the Grand Duke even acquired some of the wicked and salacious verses the painter was said to have written. They were read out to a circle of his friends to great amusement.

It was my custom to walk on down to the Ponte Sant'Angelo

and look across at the castle. I recall the word that went round about His Holiness Sixtus V. In his time the city was ravaged by bands of soldiery and hungry hordes who had been obliged to leave their homes because of famine. Sixtus took such strong measures to combat the bandits that it was said of his first years in the Chair of St Peter that: 'In that year there were more heads on stakes on the bridge than melons on the square.'

Now and again I would cross the river and continue as far as St Peter's new church in the Vatican meadows to admire the progress of the work.

For many years the finest artists have been commissioned to adorn the church – indeed, only the finest artists of the Catholic persuasion, of course. I know for certain that Merisi felt it as a terrible setback that he was not asked – *egregius in Urbe pictor!*

Finally he was given a commission, for one of the chapels. And that went wrong as well, one could say. The Palaphrenieri Brothers would not accept his *Madonna and Child with St Anne*, which as a matter of fact is a good picture. But it was sold to the papal family instead – not a bad substitute.

Permit me to remark that the relationship between a painter and his noble or ecclesiastical protector is not generally understood. The painter is seen as a mere servant, like the great man's chief chef, his astrologer or at best his treasurer. The lord commands and rewards, the servant carries out orders and is grateful.

In former times a rich and famous protector, a powerful pope or a Lorenzo de Medici, added lustre to his painter. But today an extraordinary painter can just as much add lustre to his lord.

It can be objected that this should not be so, that the God-given relationship between lord and servant should reflect the relationship between the one Lord and all His earthly under-lings, so that it is the humble duty of every servant to serve his master to the best of his capability. I have nothing to add to this.

As I mentioned, the papal family purchased a picture by Caravaggio, a picture pious monks had rejected. In almost pre-cisely the same way I myself was able to secure a picture for the Grand Duke, a *Death of the Virgin* which the Carmelites of Sta Maria della Scala were unable to use.

The Death of the Virgin is a remarkable picture, for it depicts exactly *that*. Here Maria's death is not a transition to her ascen-sion but an earthly ending. The dead face has acquired a *stiffness* and a nuance of colouring which is painted with great brilliance – and he has also managed to handle the shortened perspective of the corpse's left arm, which lies stiffly stretched out towards the viewer. True, the light is slightly too theatrical, the background dissolves into a flat darkness, and one of those ill-placed draperies Caravaggio loved to include everywhere hangs from the ceiling, quite out of context. But as a whole this is a picture which certainly enhances the Grand Duke's collection.

On the one occasion when I myself met the painter, he had just been attacked and was in a pretty bad way, from a blow to the head among other things. This must have been about six months before he had to leave Rome. At that time he spent much of his time with a somewhat slovenly elderly bookseller, from whom I had the impression that the painter for some reason or other respected almost as a father and whom he had used as a model many times. Also staying with the bookseller was a woman I easily recognized as Maria in several of the pictures. I had the feeling that somehow or other this woman felt herself responsible for the attack on the painter. But Merisi himself thought the assault had been made from quite a different motive, that it was because he had promised a wealthy and powerful man to paint the walls of his private chapel *al fresco* and had received an advance of a small fortune, said to be a matter of about 500 scudi. Since then he had tried to get out of his promise with excuses and explanations. Naturally he had used up the money.

The fact probably was that Caravaggio was simply unable to paint frescoes. Wet stucco is exacting; it demands a quick eye, a sure and relaxed technique, a cool calmness which was the last thing this painter possessed. He found foreshortened perspective difficult and often had to repaint it; even in his finished canvases there can be an extended arm pointing clumsily out into nothing.

So undoubtedly he should have refused to accept the advance. However, I have heard a curious rumour, which I have absolutely no way of confirming but which I repeat here, as – in case it should contain a grain of truth – it is not without importance to the question of the painter's guilt and responsibility.

It suggested that the bandits who assaulted the painter had been sent by the man who had paid out the advance on the frescoes. He had wanted to exercise power to back up the demand for repayment of his 500 scudi. After having been beaten up in that emphatic manner, Caravaggio decided, sensibly enough, to pay back the advance. He spent the winter contacting wealthy men and borrowing money – God knows how many canvases he had to promise before the sum was complete. Of course, news of this spread all over the city, and far too many people knew that the painter had the habit of keeping the whole of the huge sum on his person, because, with typical egoism, he felt it was more secure in his own care than with anyone else – and, besides, he always carried arms.

If the rumour is to be believed, the notorious Ranuccio knew about this large sum. He considered the painter owed him money and stopped him on the Campo Marzio to settle accounts, if necessary with force. In short: he assaulted Caravaggio sword in hand with the intention of seizing a sizeable sum. The only response from the painter was to defend himself so thoroughly that unfortunately he stabbed the bandit to death.

One may ask why Caravaggio did not claim self-defence but left the scene at once. People answer that his reputation as a drunkard and brawler was such that no one would believe him. And with a large sum of ready money to hand it was not difficult for him to leave the city.

This most probably saved his life. For the time being – because no doubt the money went with him in his flight, and he did not get the debt to his powerful commissioner paid. It may well be that somewhere an impatient banker or prince or what you will is still waiting for his 500 scudi.

The Account of Ignazio,
Municipal Clerk of Naples

I AM OBLIGED by the authorities to state what I know about the painter Merisi and his two periods of residency in our city, neither of which were of long duration – please God they had been still briefer, because this man causes nothing but discord and disturbance.

Directly he arrived in the city rumours spread that he had sought Spanish jurisdiction to avoid arrest for a murder in Rome, and confirmation of this was later brought by our envoy. But this did not stand in the way of his getting several commissions here in Naples and of a crowd of impressionable young people gathering around him, to whom it is said he gave instruction in painting at times. I know nothing about that, but his activities in teaching them to drink and follow other licentious pursuits we soon came to hear about at the City Hall.

However, he took himself off and obtained a passage to Malta. In other words, he made haste to find somewhere where he was not branded as a murderer. In due course we were sent a confidential report on his stay in those parched, scorched islands, the main details of which I shall permit myself to reproduce here, since without doubt it is of great importance regarding the question of pardon.

The painter Merisi was very well received by the Knights of St John, not least because he was able to tell them that the exemplar and patron saint of the Order, John the Baptist, was a theme for which he had a particular fondness, including the young John, the desert prophet and the adult martyr. He declared that he had a desire to be received into the order and that he would serve it through his work.

Apparently he kept his word. He painted the Grand Master's portrait, to general acclaim, and he painted a huge picture for the cathedral of Valletta – how amazing that such a village can aspire to a cathedral!

This enormous painting is said to be a horrific representation of the beheading of St John. They say that the almost naked executioner has not yet managed to completely sever the holy man's head from his body and is reaching for the dagger every executioner carries in his belt, which is called the *misericordia*,* to put an end to the martyr's suffering. Salome, that fearful woman, stands waiting close by, ready to seize her reward by the hair and set it on the dish she is to bear in triumph into the hall!

The most tasteless detail in the picture, not to say directly repellant in all its grotesque self-regard, is that the painter has inscribed his signature on it, as some self-aggrandizing picture-makers apparently have a habit of doing nowadays. And as if that

---

* Mercy. (Editor's note)

were not enough, the signature is penned out of the river of blood from the neck of the holy John that runs along the ground.

I for my part have believed that altar-pieces should provide consolation and edification and should not show detailed and graphic scenes of execution or other subjects that can frighten the life out of the congregation. But then I am only a simple town clerk and neither a painter nor a grand master.

On the basis of these and other pictures Merisi did fulfil his desire. He became an honorary knight of the Order of St John and swore to defend with his sword any danger or foe that might threaten Christendom, especially the Turks if they should ever come again as they did in the terrible year of 1565 – may the Lord and his saints prevent that ever happening. Well, there is much to indicate that this painter is probably as talented with the sword as with the brush, so he might well have chopped the head off any janissaries who attacked, if need arose.

Apparently he was proud of his honorary knighthood. One or two people even maintain he had boasted that now he could return to Rome and fight duels with certain noble persons who had previously rejected his challenges because it was beneath them to fight with a man without a title!

However, shortly after that he was not only arrested and interned in the fortress of St Elmo but also relieved of both his knight's robes and his very title. The reason for this is not clearly stated in the document I refer to, merely as 'dishonourable behaviour'.

Now, in all righteousness, it must be granted that the concepts of honour within the Order of St John are relatively strict. Moreover, one must assume that the news that their latest brother was actually a murderer would have reached an outpost like Malta some time after his arrival. That may well have been sufficient grounds. On the other hand, the words could of course cover the most scandalous actions.

I mention this last possibility for a particular reason. Not a few rumours have circulated hinting that the celibacy which is imposed on the Knights of St John leads to unmentionable relations between some brothers, obviously those who had previously shown signs of a sick and depraved nature and who should therefore never have taken the oath. For the painter got away from St Elmo, apparently through the very 'Gateway of Aid' through which wounded defenders were smuggled out during the glorious siege in the war against the heathens. On that occasion it was the Lord himself who showed the Grand Master de La Valette and his men this route to deliverance. Where Merisi's flight is concerned I am afraid that quite different forces pointed out the way of escape. The very fact that he managed to escape is absolute proof that he must have had assistants, fellow conspirators, brothers in dishonour. Anyone may speculate over the kind of shameful bonds that linked these dishonourable brothers.

The painter was transported to Sicily in a boat. He is said to have painted altar-pieces in Syracuse and Messina (some even say Palermo), commissioned by both religious orders and by the city fathers in the senate of Messina.

But then he turned up in Naples yet again. If he had been

invited here it was certainly not on the city fathers' initiative.

It is not always sufficiently recognized in Rome that Naples is a big city. The biggest in the world, some say. It is not easy to keep order in such a place. The side streets are long and narrow; they resemble ravines cutting into the mountainsides. There is endless traffic to and from the markets. Into the town stream disloyal farm labourers from the great estates; they desert their lords quite illegally without any prospects of work to go to. Instead they huddle together on the outskirts of town, build wretched mud huts and keep themselves alive by begging and worse things. Locanda del Cerriglio is a lodging house in one of these dubious districts, and whatever the painter was doing there is best kept to himself.

However it may have been, he was set upon, and pretty thoroughly. For the purpose of this account I have looked up the court documents in the case and see that the doctor describes Merisi's wounds as 'severe and open, both on the body and especially the face. The man is barely recognisable, and it will undoubtedly take a long time for him to regain his health, if he does so at all. His face will certainly be permanently disfigured.'

No light was thrown on the attack. Only bandits and petty criminals live in the area, and any one of them could have gone for the painter, merely for amusement's sake. A few vague rumours overheard by a police spy were highly contradictory and not to be relied upon. (These people are naturally notorious liars.) The rumours asserted that the assault had been ordered and paid for by an eminent personage living outside Naples.

Some thought the order came from Malta, others maintained that powerful forces in Rome were behind it.

Furthermore, the aforesaid Merisi is no longer in Naples. Some say he is travelling north to wait for a prospective pardon, others that he fled because he is afraid of a fresh attack.

That some few isolated men of the Church in our city found it opportune to commission works from this painter, despite his reputation, is up to them to answer for. I have seen two of these pictures. One is an extremely repulsive representation of how Christ was whipped. There is a kind of lingering enjoyment in this depiction of two muscular men – a third is just picking up a whip made of twigs, as if he too is about to take part in the misdeed – dancing round the suffering Lord in inflamed rage.

The other, strangely enough commissioned by the otherwise pious and charitable brothers of Pio Monte della Misericordia, purports to be a depiction of the seven good deeds of mercy. It is a sombre and highly confused picture, in which the painter has sought to squeeze everything possible on to one canvas, with the result that the viewer cannot distinguish one part of the action from another. If one looks away from the Virgin and some angels looking down on the whole scene, the effect chiefly suggests that the artist painted a chance crowd of people jammed together at the corner of the Via del Duomo and the Via Tribunali, although not even the buildings are correct. And I really have to ask what this serves: a repulsive old bearded prisoner sits behind bars. Outside on the pavement stands a young and beautiful woman who has bared one breast and *is giving suck* to the ancient through the bars! To be sure, according to the holy teaching of the Church good deeds consist both of visiting those in captivity and giving drink to those who thirst – but surely not at the same time, at least not in this highly unnatural and contrived manner.

To see that the painter has included his own portrait in this altar-piece, although in a fairly inconspicuous position, is hardly more than to be expected of such a totally disrespectful person. Well, perhaps that was wise of him, so posterity can see what he looked like before the knifing in Locanda del Cerriglio.

Finally, I should give a brief warning against attaching any credence whatever to the foolish rumours flying around of miracles taking place before this loathsome altar-piece. Only ignorant and superstitious women from the poorest quarters of the town delude themselves into believing such things. These mothers pray unceasingly for their reprobate sons and daughters, for they undoubtedly have reason to do so. But if some soul or other is saved from drink, thieving and prostitution, it is more likely due to the hard-working city police and resolute judicial system. From the foolish votive offerings that are brought in one can easily understand that it is all fantasy: clumsy portrayals of the whipped Magdalene, false weights no longer used by the swindler, even daggers which for all I know have been wielded to commit murder but which now are cast aside for ever. In my opinion this offensive habit serves not at all to further the honour of the God-fearing brothers of Pio Monte.

The Account of
Ottaviano Gabrelli, Bookseller

TRUTH WILL CONQUER.

During the past few weeks I have had the pleasure in my small bookshop of selling the short publication entitled *Siderius Nuncius* or the Messenger of the Stars, printed in Venice, a little pamphlet of twenty-four pages in modest octavo format. It was written by a Professor Galileo. The professor has made himself a wonderful new instrument, it is said according to the instructions of a Dutch optician, which he calls *telescopus*. The instrument not only enables the greatly despised human senses to realize their full potential – it improves vision enormously, so that now everyone can see what was previously hidden from even the most learned!

Through his *telescopus* the professor has seen a sight that has never before been seen, nay, never even so much as *imagined*. He has observed that Jupiter has four moons.

Truth will conquer. Did Aristotle say anything about Jupiter's moons? Definitely not. Ptolemy? Never. Not even Bruno at the stake would have dreamed of Jupiter's moons, no more than his judges would have dared to conceive of the idea.

But Jupiter does have four moons.

It may be said that this has nothing at all to do with Merisi, the painter from Caravaggio, but it most certainly has. Caravaggio is the Galileo of the canvas. He does not rely on anything but his own sight, and it is this, above all, that has caused his difficulties. Indeed, I think it was precisely this that led to his misfortune. So then if the professor can write about his moons, the painter must be able to paint what *he* sees: human bodies, their flesh – he cannot create anything based on entrenched traditions in antiquated old books.

A story is going around Rome about how two other astronomers flatly refused to look into the instrument, horrified they might have to discover that Jupiter actually does have moons. Is this not reminiscent of how the priests refused to *look* at the painter's truths: the dirty feet of a shabby apostle, the dead Maria, Doubting Thomas?

Truth will conquer. I took the girl Lena into my house purely and simply in an attempt to shield my friend Caravaggio from yet more pestering, whatever others may have thought and said about my motives.

I have never believed the story that the painter had mistreated the two women on the Corso, the fruiterer and her daughter. It is true that he was hotheaded and prone to fly off the handle at that time, but he was not accustomed to use force on people he considered of no consequence.

The fact is that my valued friend was the victim of a conspiracy, this was what led to his misfortune. Lena Antognetti was a mere pawn in that affair, and I, for my part, do not believe either that Gaspare Albertini, the notary, was the person really behind it all – he was, with due respect, too stupid for that.

What is certain is that I took Lena into my house to save them both and for no other reason. Anyone who doubts this can ask that honest citizen Prospero Orsi, the artist, who was also in court to mediate and resolve the case in this way. And this was why I was probably the one who had most to do with Caravaggio in the year before he was obliged to flee from here.

First, it must be said that the aim of this conspiracy was of course the killing of my friend. The reason for selecting Ranuccio Tomassoni to incite Caravaggio to a duel was that they must all have been convinced that Ranuccio would have no trouble defeating the artist. He was a trained guardsman, who had been in the service of various high-ranking men, well known for both armed combat and hand-to-hand fighting. When he had dispatched Caravaggio he would be able to explain the whole thing as single combat, a duel, or even to plead self-defence, and have ample opportunity to seek protection from the great men he had served, the Farnese family, for instance, or the Aldobrandini.

They made thorough preparations. A few days earlier Ranuccio and Caravaggio had played *pallacorda* at the sports ground on the Campo Marzio, and they had naturally quarrelled in the course of the contest.

It was a crafty plan which should have succeeded. To provoke the painter to such fury that he drew his sword was no great problem. A practised swordsman prepared for combat *should* easily beat an excitable, intoxicated painter even if the painter is known to handle his weapon with a certain dexterity. It will happen nine times out of ten, forty-nine times out of fifty.

But this was either the fiftieth time, or Caravaggio was a better swordsman than anyone had suspected. The victim triumphed over his murderer but paid with his life by flight and exile.

Who knows, this might have formed part of the calculations. Even if against all probability the painter won, *he* would not be able to seek refuge with any protector. His list of sins was too long to be able to carry a man's death as well. No del Monte, Giustiniani or Cherubini would be able to smooth over that. The fact is – and it is known only to me and a few others – that he sought shelter in the house of Cardinal Colonna, whom the artist's father had served at some time. But even this mighty family could not do more than get the painter out of town and hide him on their country estate for a few weeks. (He expressed his gratitude to the cardinal by painting a masterly *Magdalene in Ecstasy*, which, incidentally, exhibits Lena's unmistakeable features.)

In short, even though the planned murder was unsuccessful, they were rid of Michel Angelo Merisi, now known to everyone as Caravaggio.

The question arises: who were *they*? I have been expressly assured that the account I give here will serve only its proper purpose and in no way can be used against my person. It is only with this categorical proviso that I note down the following ideas.

I see two possibilities.

The first is that one of his former wealthy patrons has turned against him. No one can make me suggest names. In favour of such a possibility is the fact that the Tomassoni brothers had contacts in the best families and were known for their robust brutality. Indeed, to be sure, if *I* were a cardinal or banker or high-standing statesman and wished to have such an assignment carried out, I would apply to none other than such men.

But why should some or other of the leading men in town desire the life of an artist? I really do not know, but I do not think rich and powerful men are very different from others. It might be caused by jealousy: it is well known that obsessed collectors set greater store by their collection than almost anything else. The painter might have accepted a commission from some or other Reverence. Then later he might have received an offer of a higher fee from another collector and painted the picture for this competitor instead; it would be just like him.

We know how much time and money these men expend in getting themselves the best collections. The Duke of Mantua, who has to stay at home in his own little duchy at least some of the time and is therefore fearful of missing what is going on here in Rome, employed his own spy, a budding young Flemish painter. It was *he* who bought up *The Death of the Virgin* when the Carmelites took fright and refused to hang the picture. Duke Gonzaga was so unreasonably proud of his trophy that he arranged a public exhibition of the painting in Rome before taking it back to Mantua. It was said that the picture had already aroused such a sensation among artists that it was absolutely necessary for it to be exhibited, but may it not just as well have been in order to celebrate a triumph over a rival?

Or think of a great collector, a real benefactor, who has collected numerous paintings by a painter over a long period during which the wealthy man supported and helped the painter in other ways. But then two things occur simultaneously. The rich man's affairs take a downturn, he can no longer ladle out money. In contrast, the painter makes great strides. New commissions come pouring in and he no longer needs the friend and helper who kept him alive when times were really hard.

Then does not such a man, once so powerful, have a double reason for desiring the life of his painter? Not only is he left thankless for his beneficence, he must with other ignominies watch his protégé go to the new men basking in glory and honour. Yet he does have *something* left – the paintings. Now with paintings, as with everything else, value depends on two things. Of course that which is beautiful and well executed is valuable. But that which is, in addition, *exceptional* is even more valuable.

A living painter works like one possessed and produces still more paintings.

Well, this was one of my possibilities, that a rich and powerful collector was the long shadow who actually drew the sword out of Ranuccio's sheath.

The second possibility I am even more reluctant to mention and shall do so only with the greatest brevity.

There exist organisations that work to spread the Faith, about which it is said that they do not hold back from using certain means to achieve their object. I emphasize that this is something said and not anything I personally go along with.

Then, was the artist such a danger to the Faith that he had to be eliminated or perhaps forced to flee? I do not know. But certain it is that there is a physicality in his paintings, the like of which has never been seen. These mortifying monks do not seem to find any place for the fleshly in the faith they wish so fervently to spread; it is as if they fear the flesh more than the Devil himself.

This must be an illusion engendered by that same Devil. For if I am not mistaken, it is written: 'And the Word became flesh and dwelt amongst us.'

It is this flesh that Merisi from Caravaggio painted. He painted *Doubting Thomas* as if the apostle had been an inquisitive peasant from the Campagna; indeed, he painted the flesh of Jesus to appear so palpable and real in a manner that would be hard to better – or to worsen. Jesus draws back his robe, Thomas leans close to the gaping wound in his side and *thrusts his finger into the Lord's body.*

Christ uncovers His naked flesh, so that even I, who unfortunately am not one of the most enthusiastic in the Faith, felt a stab of physical aversion at this scene, at seeing the Lord's body, that holiest and most spiritual of all material objects, made fleshly in this brutal, almost obscene way.

But all the painter has done, of course, is to follow the words of Scripture to the letter: 'Reach hither thy finger, and thrust it into my side, and be not faithless but believing!' If the general public is given access to this painting, every ignorant sinner will be able to see with his own eyes that although the Word was made flesh, it was thereby made holy in all its imperfection – for the Lord is not only spirit but also physical, vulnerable body.

In no way would I openly accuse our sacred orders and congregations for wishing to take the life of a painter because he demonstrates a truth which *they* cannot bear to look upon. On the other hand, I also remember Giordano Bruno. He paid dear at the stake on the Campo de'Fiori for the truths a few people could not bear.

And I happen to know that there are members of those orders who were earlier well acquainted with Caravaggio the painter, who are familiar with his violent moods. These are persons who know all the details of his undesirable habits where drink and gambling are concerned. It would be simple for them to stage such a scene.

But perhaps I am mistaken, perhaps after all it was merely the revenge of the foolish notary.

Postscript by
Innocenzo Promontorio

And David took the head of the Philistine and brought it to
Jerusalem.

THE NEWS OF the death of the painter Michel Angelo Merisi da
Caravaggio at Port'Ercole has just reached town, and it has rendered completely invalid the whole of the long account I finished
writing only a few weeks ago and sent to the Curia.

Nevertheless, for my own part, and not least because it is
possible that these documents may have a place in his posthu-
mous reputation, I should like to add this: the report of his death
is extremely confused and contradictory; indeed, I cannot
express it otherwise. It is *ambiguous.* This is what it claims to
have taken place.

When Michel arrived at the Spanish outpost of Port'Ercole,
he took his scanty belongings – among them a new painting –
down to the shore, where he had arranged for a felucca to pick
him up. No one knows where he had intended to go, but there are
murmurs regarding an eminent protector who wanted to shelter
him on his estates until the case for a pardon had been concluded.

Then the police arrived.

Did they take him for a French spy or an agitator? Some say this. Others state he had picked a quarrel with an innkeeper who had him arrested, others again that he had molested a young woman – or a young lad.

But there is yet another explanation for this last arrest of his. If *this* is correct, it may be the only time out of all those when the police took this man into custody that he was totally innocent.

They say he was mistaken for another. Because they say that his face was so disfigured that he was unrecognizable.

But I do not understand how he could be mistaken for someone else, unless another disfigured person was in the neighbourhood. I myself believe rather that the explanation for his arrest was *on account of* his appearance, if, that is, it is really true that his face was so badly damaged. A half-witted policeman may well have concluded that such an outlandish person should be arrested for safety's sake. The scars on his face must obviously have been the result of a criminal act.

He was released after a day or two, but then the felucca had left – and taken his belongings with it.

He fell ill with a fever, probably because of the black bile that must have been ravaging his body after such an idiotic occurrence. He ran about the beach in the blazing July sunshine searching for the boat that was to collect him, became delirious – and died alone, with neither priest nor confession to comfort him.

But at least his last painting was recovered. It arrived in

Rome with some other possessions. I have had an opportunity to see it. The young David is yet another of those slim, beautiful lads, less naked it is true, only half his chest is revealed. There is more reflection than triumph in the boy's face. His right hand is obscured by the theatrical darkness, only his sword flashes with oblique virility within the picture. In his left hand he holds Goliath's big head by the hair. The Philistine's face still expresses vivid astonishment at what has happened, while the blood slowly drips from the severed throat.

This is Michel's very last picture, in which the painter and the painted melt together: the face of Goliath is that of Michel. The eyes about to burst are *his* beautiful eyes; he has captured them in the transition between life and extinction.

What other artist has painted *this* motif? David with his sling is a favoured theme, David and Saul, not to mention David and Bathsheba. But he alone has hit upon the brief comment on the head of the Philistine. And who else in all the world has painted a 'Self-Portrait as the Decapitated Philistine'?

The Vatican has questioned me on the truth concerning Michel Angelo Merisi da Caravaggio, and I tried to give an adequate answer in the account I previously presented. But perhaps I was mistaken, perhaps it was not only this urge towards self-assertiveness, this consecrating of his own senses and imperfect thoughts, that brought the misfortunes upon him.

At one time the artist and I loved the same woman. Usually this turns men into the bitterest of enemies. But when she died in the most frightful manner, her death bound us together in a friendship which held both intense light and deep shadows within it.

I believe the sight of Beatrice Cenci's face pursued him for eleven years. In the end it blended with his own, and this face assumed the features of the dead Goliath.

But there is one thing I shall never understand: Why did he have to commemorate our one-time friendship by giving *my* face to the young, victorious David with his sword?

Editor's Postscript

MUCH OF THE material appearing in these accounts is found in part in other sources, as are most of the writers of the accounts.

The architect Onorio Longhi was well known in his time, not least because after his pardon in 1611 he returned to Rome and became the architect of the church of SS Ambrogio e Carlo on the Corso, a position he assumed in 1612 and retained until his death (from syphilis) in 1619, when the post was taken over by his son Martino.

The painter's brother, Giovan Battista Merisi, is known only for the settlement he himself mentions in his account.

Phyllida Melandroni appears in contemporary sources. She is mentioned as model for several pictures, among them a *Portrait of Phyllida Melandroni,* now missing.

The painter Prospero Orsi and the bookseller Ottaviano Gabrelli appear in several contemporary documents, both in cases in the civil court and in documents of a criminal type, whose broad detail seems to corroborate their descriptions of the external circumstances concerning Caravaggio's life in Rome. There is a very thorough treatment of these documents in, for instance, the book by Riccardo Bassani and Fiora Bellini, *Caravaggio assassino*.

Lena Antognetti's name appears in the report presented by the notary, Mariano Pasqualoni, accusing Caravaggio of assault 'with a sword or a large knife' in the summer of 1605. Here the context is somewhat uncertain – was Pasqualoni acting in some way or other on behalf of his colleague Gaspare Albertini? Lena's account – which was obviously dictated to a scribe – is sometimes obscure and strongly subjective. But it is supported to a certain extent by the fact that the model for the *Madonna of Loreto* and Maria in *The Madonna and Child with St Anne* is clearly the same woman.

Rubens's sojourn in Italy has been previously documented in minute detail.

It is extremely tempting, given this background, to assume that these accounts *are* authentic documents utilized in the work of the Curia on Caravaggio's plea for pardon.

However, there is one considerable drawback. The person whose account forms the most substantial part of the material, Innocenzo Promontorio, has left no trace of himself in any contemporary source. He does not appear in any proceedings of the criminal court in which the names of Michel Angelo Merisi and Onorio Longhi turn up so many times. Nor do the well-preserved rolls of the University of Padua record any such student for the years in question. What is worse, the town he expressly names as his birthplace, Frassinocasa, does not seem to exist.

His account indicates that he is attached to the Society of

Jesus. But the editor's requests to examine the archives of the order with a view to finding Innocenzo Promontorio and ascertain his position within the Society were refused.

There seem to be only two possible explanations:

Innocenzo's account may be pure fabrication. Since it is not separated out in any way from the other accounts in the archive, such a conclusion must cast serious doubt on the authenticity of the whole collection.

The other possibility is that this account is a more or less fictionalized presentation, penned by a person who actually did know the painter well but who for some reason could not write a report under his own name. If this is the case, this person must be a well-educated man of high standing.

But any speculations of this kind must be mere guesswork. It would not be right to draw any definitive conclusion.

Moreover, it has not been possible to verify the existence of a town clerk in Naples by the name of Ignazio at the period in question. But it must be noted that the archives for Naples are not as well preserved as the corresponding documents for the City of Rome and the Holy See. Ignazio's information on Caravaggio's stay in Naples and on Malta agree in the main with that attested to in other sources.

Concluding Unscholarly Comment
by the Editor

SO MANY EXPLANATIONS, so many versions, so many stories that overlap, misplace, contradict and annul each other.

That ought not to worry me. I write this towards the very end of the second millennium AD, a period when uncertainty is the basis of everything, when philosophers are not engaged in discovering the truth but in proving that Truth is in principle inaccessible, that there is nothing to be found but small, subjective and incompatible truths.

These accounts of the truculent artist Merisi, the murderer from Caravaggio, seem both in themselves and seen in their incomprehensible context to substantiate this view. The events of his life lose contour, dissolve away, vanish into thin air. Every attempt to establish an *understanding* is annihilated by the next statement.

I began work on this publication in search of a certain clarity. It was, of course, my interest in the art, ideas and social history of the seventeenth century that prompted it, but if I may be permitted a remark of a private nature: I was driven also by personal need.

It was the need to describe and comprehend *holiness*. This could also be expressed as the wish to reconstruct this lost power, which we no longer understand and which thus causes large areas of our history to have become incomprehensible to us.

This need has not been fulfilled through the work on the text. For what have I made of it? Footnotes! My contribution to the understanding of the course and motive power of history is a series of pedantic little comments, dry information at the furthest margin of a story dealing with life and death.

But the text's refusal to reveal its secrets is a fate all editors must take into account. And perhaps I might have accepted it as a reasonable, indeed, necessary ending to my work, had it not been for one single fact: *Caravaggio's pictures exist*. The altarpieces depicting the murderer, the drunkard, the troublemaker, the abuser of women are free for all to see, in S. Luigi dei Francesi, Sta Maria del Popolo, Sant'Agostino, Pio Monte in Naples, the Church of St John in Valletta, in other churches and numerous galleries.

The accounts I have found and reproduced are interwoven with a fundamental ambiguity. But the paintings shine with transcendental authority.

The pictures speak or, what is even more disquieting, they are spoken through.

Rome
April 1997

155

Select Sources

Bassani, Ricardo and Fiora Bellini, *Caravaggio assassino*, Rome, 1994

Calveri, Maurinio, Caravaggio, in the series 'Art dossier' No. 1-1986

Dell'Acqua, G.A. and M. Cinotti, *Il Caravaggio e le sue grande opere da S. Luigi dei Francesi*, Milan, 1971

Gregori, Mina (ed.), *Caravaggio: Come nascono i Capolavori*, Milan, 1991

Hibbart, H., *Caravaggio*, London, 1981

Januszcak, Waldemar, *Techniques of the World's Great Painters*, QED Publishing, 1980

Kindlers Malerei Lexikon, Munich, 1985

Ravaglioli, Armando, *Breve storia di Roma*, in the economy series Tascabili economici Newton, Rome, 1994

Zuffi, Stefano, *Caravaggio*, Milan, 1991

CD-ROM *Caravaggio* in the series CD ROM ARTE, 1996. Series published by Giunti Multimedia and *La Repubblica*.

In addition, it is a great pleasure to acknowledge one of the best books – regardless of genre – I know, with which I have had a relationship for many years, Arthur Koestler's *The Sleepwalkers: A History of Man's Changing Vision of the Universe*, London, 1959 (I have used the Penguin edition of 1977).

But above all – naturally – the paintings. Here is a selection of the most important:

Rome

San Luigi dei Francesi

Vocazione di S. Matteo	(The Calling of St Matthew)
S. Matteo e l'Angelo[*]	(St Matthew and the Angel)
Martirio di S. Matteo	(The Martyrdom of St Matthew)

Sta Maria del Popolo

Conversione di S. Paolo	(The Conversion of St Paul)
Crocifissione di S. Pietro	(The Crucifixion of St Peter)

Sant'Agostino

Madonna dei pellegrini/Madonna di Loreto	(Madonna of Loreto)

Galleria Borghese

Ragazzo con canestro di frutta	(Boy with a Basket of Fruit)

[*] This is the second version of the picture. The first, rejected, was destroyed during the bombing of Berlin in 1945.

Doubting Thomas

Bacchino malato	(Little Bacchus in Sickness)
Madonna dei Palafrenieri	(Madonna of the Palafrenieri)
S. Girolamo scrivente	(St Jerome in His Study)
David con la testa di Golia	(David with the Head of Goliath)

Galleria Doria Pamphilj

Riposo nella fuga in Egitto	(The Rest on the Flight into Egypt)
Maddalena penitente	(The Penitent Magdalene)

Pinacoteca Capitolina

La buona ventura	(The Gypsy Fortune Teller)
S. Giovanni Battista	(St John the Baptist)

Galleria Nazionale d'Arte Antica, Palazzo Barberini

Narciso	(Narcissus)
Giuditta che decapita Oloferne	(Judith and Holofernes)

Vatican Museums

Sepoltura di Cristo	(The Entombment of Christ)

Naples

Museo di Capodimonte

Flagellazione	(The Flagellation of Christ)
Martirio di sant' Ursula	(The Martyrdom of St Ursula)

Pio Monte della Misericordia

Sette opere di misericordia	(The Seven Acts of Mercy)

Florence

Galleria degli Uffizi

Medusa	(Medusa)
Bacco	(Bacchus)
Il Sacrificio di Isacco	(The Sacrifice of Isaac)

Milan

Pinacoteca Ambrosiana

Canestro di frutta	(Basket of Fruit)

Pinacoteca di Brera

Cena in Emmaus	(Supper at Emmaus)

Messina

Museo Regionale

Resurrezione di Lazzaro	(The Resurrection of Lazarus)
Adorazione dei pastori	(Adoration of the Shepherds)

Syracuse

Sta Lucia
    Sepoltura di Sta Lucia   (The Burial of Saint Lucy)

Valletta

St John's Co-Cathedral
    Decollazione del Battista   (The Beheading of St John the Baptist)
    S. Girolamo scrivente   (Saint Jerome Writing)

Paris

Louvre
    La buona ventura   (The Gypsy Fortune Teller)
    Morte della Vergine/Morte della Madonna   (The Death of the Virgin)
    Ritratto di Alof de Wignacourt   (Portrait of Alof de Wignacourt)

London

National Gallery
    Cena in Emmaus   (Supper at Emmaus)
    Giovane morso da un ramarro[*]   (Boy Bitten by a Lizard)

Madrid

Thyssen-Bornemisza Collection
    Sta Caterina d'Alessandria   (St Catherine of Alexandria)

Berlin

Staatliche Museen Preussischer Kulturbesitz
    Amor vittorioso   (Love Victorious)

Potsdam-Sanssoucis Bildergallerie
    Incredulità di S. Tommaso   (Doubting Thomas)

There are also works by Caravaggio in Dublin, St Petersburg, Vienna and Genoa as well as in Fort Worth, Texas, Cleveland, Ohio and Hartford, Connecticut. Other works have also been credited to him, some on uncertain grounds, e.g. the version of *Abraham and Isaac* in Princeton, New Jersey.

A.N.

---

* A version of this picture is also to be found in Florence. Whether one of them is a copy or Caravaggio painted both is a vexed question among art historians.